THE GATES
OF HELL'S WIDE OPEN

THE FATE OF MAN IS IN MICHAEL'S HANDS

RONALD TURNER

Library of Congress Control Number: 2025903953

ISBN
979-8-89641-047-8 (Paperback)
979-8-89641-048-5 (eBook)
979-8-89641-046-1 (Hardcover)

FOREWORD

It is written by man, by the authority of GOD, that one day the Heavens will send forth the son of GOD. This day has already come and gone, and yet man was too blind to see. It is also written, that GOD cast out an angel whom disobeyed him. He cursed this angel, and he placed him into the bowels of the Earth to rule over all that are evil. The place in which GOD cast him is known to all as "Hell". And the angel whom was named Lucifer, made a promise to GOD. He promised that one day he would take his revenge upon Heaven by destroying his creation. GOD had plans to assure that he would be kept where he belonged. GOD placed a golden gate at the entrance of Hell and sent an army of angels to protect the gate from ever being opened. But even with the army of angels; one has managed to slip by. And he the most evil of all; even more evil than Lucifer; swore to rule over the earth.

CHAPTER

1

Michael Talon was a troubled child. Not troubled as in a child who is criminally troubled but more troubled in mind and spirit. He had dreams of past events of different time periods all the way back to the birth of Christ and before. Michael told his mother about his dreams but she always told him to stop telling stories.

He felt alone and unloved by his mother almost as if she wasn't his real mother. His father had died before he was born, so he couldn't talk to him about his dreams. His brother listened to him and always told him that he believed him. His grand mother was the kind of woman who was a loving kind and gentile woman. She told him that all things which we dream have a meaning to them.

He didn't really understand what his grandmother meant by it, but listened just the same. She told him that the dreams he'd dreamed were that of past events of past lives. He was scared because of some of the things he'd seen in his dreams. He told his grandmother that he'd seen GOD in his dreams and he told him,

"Not to fear but to rejoice."

He didn't know what was meant by what he'd said to him and asked her if she did. She smiled at him and told him to come and sit on her lap. He walked over to her and turned around; she reached down and picked him up. She put him on her lap and reached over to the plate of cookies. She picked up a cookie and handed it to him. He took the cookie and looked up at her with a smile on his face. She kissed him on the forehead and said,

"Well Michael; you have been blessed by the Lord with something of great importance. And he has a plan for your life that you must be willing to fore fill."

He looked at his grandmother with skepticism on his face and felt goose bumps all over. He wasn't sure what his grand mother was saying to him after all he was only 5 at the time. He looked at her and turned around to give her a hug. He squeezed her and told her in an innocent childish squeeze. She smiled at him and put her arms around him and hugged him back. He told her,

"I love you very, very much grandma!" she squeezed him even tighter and said,

"I love you too!" He smiled at her and slid off of her lap and looked up at her. She smiled at him and she just seemed to fad out of his sight. He got up and looked for his grandmother but couldn't find her. He looked at the chair she was sitting in and seen that it was dust covered. He yelled for his grandmother but she didn't answer. He looked at the plate sitting on the table and seen it was also covered with dust. He couldn't understand where his grandmother was and why she wouldn't answer him.

His mother came running up the stairs into the attic. She started yelling at him,

"Why are you yelling for your grandmother Michael? You know she been dead for the last two years, I told you that." He started crying and ran down the stairs. He ran so fast that before he knew it, he was standing outside in the yard. He looked up to the sky crying,

"Why grandma, why did you go away? You're the only one who ever loved me, why did you leave me?"

His mother came down the stairs and opened the screen door. She stood on the porch looking at him with a look of anger on her face. She walked down the stairs and over to him, grabbing him so tight around the arm when she yanked him she almost broke his arm. She had a look on her face that would scare a grown man. She kneeled down in front of him, with anger in her voice she yelled at him telling him,

"That's enough Michael; I can't take it anymore." Michael stood there crying even more,

"Your stories; your lies; and now saying that your grandmother was in the attic. I; I just don't what to do with you anymore." She shook her head and let his arm go then just got up and walked away. She stormed up the stairs slamming the screen door behind her. Michael ran into the house and up the stairs and into his bedroom. He slammed the door behind him a jumped into bed pulling the covers over top of his head. He cried so much that he couldn't hear what his mother was doing down stairs.

His brother came into the room and tapped him on the shoulder. He pulled the cover from over his head and looked at his brother. His brother Johnny, seen his mother run into the house from the top of the stairs and pick up the phone. He was scared and hid out of her sight so she wouldn't get mad at him for seeing her in a rage. He knew better than to let her see him in a rage of anger. She's an alcoholic and a drug abuser who always took out her frustration on him if she seen him when she was angry about something.

He told him about the phone call she made when she stormed into the house. He ask him,

"Why was mommy so mad at you that she was talking to someone on the phone about you?"

He sat up and looked at Johnny; the tears were still trickling down his face. He had a scared look on his face. Johnny seen the way he was fidgeting as he sat there crying. He was so upset he was gasping breaths as he cried. Johnny had tears start trickling for him because he just knew that his mother was going to beat his brother. Johnny heard the sound of glass breaking down stairs, "crash." Then he heard her arguing with herself in an alcoholic rage,

"Stupid son of a bitch, always trying to ruin my life. You got me pregnant then you up and fucking die on me. I hate you; I'm glad you died the same as your bastard son."

Johnny started getting real scared for his brother. He thought his mother was going to kill him and wanted to protect him. The way she was going off down stairs he knew that there mother would really hurt him. Johnny heard her come up the stairs and go into his room. She was still cussing and throwing things around. Johnny grabbed Michael and got him down on the floor.

She left Johnny's room and just before she came into Michael's room, Johnny got Michael and him under the bed. She came in the room in a rage of anger looking for Michael. She was throwing his toys against the walls and cussing. They were so scared they stayed under the bed until she gave up and left slamming the door behind her. Johnny got out from under the bed and told Michael to "stay put" until he seen where their mother went. He went over to the door and slowly cracked open the door just enough to see down the hall. He saw her go into her bedroom and slam the door behind her. He looked back over to Michael and told him,

"Ok; she went into her room; she'll be passed out soon. I don't think she'll remember any of this tomorrow." Michael got out from under the bed and walked over to Johnny. They stood next to each other watching to see if she wasn't coming out of her room. After about 5 or 10 minutes went by, they left Michael's room and went into Johnny's room. They didn't hear a sound from their mother's room, so they knew she was passed out. They got up into Johnny's bed and laid there with the covers up to their necks until they fell asleep.

The next morning Michael woke up in his own bed. He didn't know how he got there or when but he was there just the same. He looked around his room to see that everything was back in its place and his room was clean. He thought that he must have dreamed that everything that happened last night was only a dream. His mother came into the room in a dress; she was carrying a bed tray with breakfast for him. Michael sat up and yawned. Whipping the sleep from his eyes, his mother sat the tray down over his lap.

She said in a tone of voice as if nothing had happened last night,

"Good morning sweetheart; and how did you sleep last night? Well I hope." She walked over and looked out of the window just as a car pulled up in front of the house into the driveway. She looked over at him with a smile on her face and said to him in a calm voice,

"Sweetheart hurry and finish up; I have a very big surprise for you."

He hurried up and ate his food then whipped his mouth with his napkin. His mother walked back over and picked up the tray. He looked to see her wearing makeup which he'd not seen her wear in a while.

"Makeup mom; you haven't wore makeup in a while. What's the special occasion?" She just smiled and said in a very sweet voice, the kind of voice that would make you kind of sick in the stomach,

"Well; I told you I have a surprise for you more like for all of us. Sweetheart please get up and get dressed and don't forget to brush your teeth wash your face and brush your hair." Then she walked out of his room closing the door behind her. He got up and got dressed and went into his bathroom to brush his teeth and hair. When he finished he took a wash cloth and washed his face and cleaned the crusty film from his eyes. He looked in the mirror and seen his grandmother standing behind him. She had a smile on her face, the same smile she had on her face upstairs in the attic yesterday. She told him not to worry about anything; she'd be with him always no matter where he is or for how long he was there. Then just as in the attic, she'd vanished. He closed his eyes and just stood there.

Johnny rushed into the room all excited and went into Michael's bathroom. He looked at Michael and asked him,

"Michael; why are you dressed and whom are those guys downstairs?" He looked at Johnny and ran past him over to the window. He saw a car sitting in the driveway. He looked back at Johnny while holding the curtains apart,

"Johnny; I can't read what's on that car in the driveway." Johnny walked over to the window and looked at the car. He squinted but it was too hard to see the words on the side of the car. The sun was shinning on the car making it hard to make out the writing. What he could make out didn't make any sense to him. Johnny walked over to the bed and sat down on the edge. He looked at Michael and told him,

"Michael; come away from the window." But Michael being curious, wanted to see if he could see where the car was from or if he knew who owned it.

While Michael was standing at the window his mother came into the room with two men dressed in military uniforms. Johnny jumped up from the bed and ran over to Michael and put his back against him and putting his arms out to protect him from the two men. Their mother bent over putting her hands on her knees and looking at Michael she said,

"Sweetie!" looking over at the two men she winked at them then looked back at Michael. And licked her lips,

"Sweetie; these two gentlemen are going to take you on a trip. They are going to take you to a place that your daddy went a long time ago when he was your age." She stood back up and turned towards the two of them and put a folded piece of paper in their top pocket of their dress jacket. She winked and liced her lips at them and sashayed out of the room keeping their attention focused on her. She turned around and leaned back against the railing pulling her dress up past her waist and putting her foot up on the chair against the wall. She didn't have any panties on she looked at them and said,

"Take care of my problem, and any time you need your problem taken care of like I did for you, call me and come over." She smiled at them and put her foot down. She took off her dress and sashayed slowly away from them. They watched her as she walked into her bed room and closed the door. They looked at each other then back at Michael and told him,

"Son come with us and we'll treat you like one of our own." But Johnny wasn't going to let them take him without a fight. Michael was crying as his brother was grabbed and held while Michael was taken by force kicking and screaming. After they'd gotten Michael out of his room Johnny was tossed onto the bed and the one who held him shut the door behind him and locked the door. Michael's mother opened the door and stood there nude as the man that had Michael passed by her leaned over and kissed her. He winked at her and told her,

"I'll call you later; I have some friends who'd like to get in on some of your action." She smiled and grabbed the other man pulling him to her she put his hand between her legs and kissed him. She pulled away like a tease and told him,

"Come back later and I'll show you some one on one appreciation for taking care of my problem." He smiled and joined his friend who was already at the car waiting with the doors locked so he couldn't get out. As they started to drive away, the passenger who was the one who locked Johnny in the bedroom looked up to see her standing with her breasts pressed against the window glass. He kept his eyes on her until he couldn't see her anymore.

His friend who was driving had a laugh in his voice as he smacked him on the arm with his finger tips,

"What did you think about the bonus we got and are going to keep on getting for taking this brat off of her hands?" He had a smile on his face as he sat there thinking about her and what she said to him when he was with her after his friend went outside. He looked back at Michael who was crying in the back seat. He couldn't see where they were going because the windows were dark tinted and the front seats were high backed seats. He said in a calm voice,

"High Michael; my name is Private Barstow it's nice to meet you. I know what your first name is but I don't know what you last name is." But Michael sat there quiet and upset that his mother lied to him. He knew that he wasn't going home and that he wouldn't see his brother again. The feeling of helplessness was something he knows oh so well, and that's how he feels at this time. Private Barstow felt as if he'd deceived Michael and he felt like a lire. Michael wiped the tears from his face and looked at private Barstow, he was thinking that he was a snake for what he'd done.

They pulled up in to the gate house of the George Patton Military Academy. The guard walked up to the car and the driver rolled down the window. He heard him speaking but couldn't make out what he was saying. The guard smiled and looked back at Michael. The smile was that of someone who just hit the jackpot in the lottery. The guard back away and saluted as the car started moving again. The driveway was long, so long he felt as if he was on his way to his execution. When the car stopped they were in front of the main building. The driver got out of the car and walked up to where a man was standing in the doorway. They looked as if they were arguing for a few minutes.

Private Barstow turned to Michael, he felt ashamed and felt as if he owed him some kind of an apology. He looked at Michael with guilt and felt that there was some kind of connection between them but didn't know what it was. He looked over at the driver and felt disgusted about what he'd done. He thought about

Michael's mother and didn't know how to tell him that they had a one night stand several months before he was born. But he kept quiet about it and felt it would be best that he never finds out about it. The reason why he felt that it was best that way is that he wasn't sure if Michael was his son.

The driver and the other man finished arguing they shook hands. As he walked back over to the car, private Barstow turned back around and faced forwards. The driver leaned in through the driver side window and told private Barstow,

"You're off duty in about ten minutes, I'll take care of this brat you go ahead and secure the car and go home." He looked back at Michael then back at the driver,

"Yes sir sergeant, anything you say sir." Private Barstow opened his door and got out of the car. He walked around the back of the car to the other side where the sergeant was standing with the back door open. Michael was sitting in the car refusing to get out of the back seat. He had his arms crossed tightly pouting and saying "no" when he was ordered by the sergeant to get out of the car. Private Barstow looked at the sergeant,

"Woo, woo sergeant if you want a kid this young to do as you want him to, you have to speak to him like a kid not a soldier." The sergeant threw his hands up in the air and backed away from the car door.

Private Barstow kneeled down in front of Michael and smiled at him. He was thinking about how his father would get him to do as he wanted and not to make him feel like a slave. A kind word usually worked and made him think that he was loved and needed. Not like he was expected to do what he wanted right then and there. He held out his hand to Michael. Michael still had his arms crossed, he looked at private Barstow. His face was swollen from crying so much. His eyes puffed at the bottom and he felt as if he was all alone.

He unfolded his arms and reached out his hand. He had a feeling that private Barstow cared for him because of the way he'd spoken to him earlier in the car while the sergeant was arguing with the other man in the doorway. Private Barstow took him by the hand and Michael got out of the car. He hugged private Barstow and held on to him like a son hugging his father. Private Barstow held on to him and felt a feeling he'd never felt before. The feeling was a calm and soothing feeling. Michael let him go and looked at him; he had a feeling that there was something about him but didn't what it was. At the same time private Barstow had the same feeling.

Private Barstow looked at Michael and started thinking that there was something familiar about him. He started putting two and two together and realized that the way he looked was like he looked when he was five. He didn't say anything to Michael about it until he knew one hundred percent that he was his father. He smiled and told Michael,

"Michael I want you to go with the sergeant and be a good boy. I'll be back later to check on you, ok." Michael looked up at the sergeant and then back at private Barstow. He shook his head yes and reached up taking him by the hand. The sergeant looked at private Barstow and asked,

"How; how did you get him to do what you said?" He looked at him with a smirk on his face,

"You just have to know how to treat kids like people; not like they're little soldiers. Treat them with respect; they'll respect you enough to do what you want." The sergeant sighed and looked down at Michael as if he was a kid himself. He asked Michael,

"We'll son; would you like to go see your room?" Michael looked up and shook his head yes. The sergeant looked at private Barstow and turned to walk away. Michael turned and waved bye to private Barstow. He closed the back door and opened the driver's side door. Private Barstow climbed into the driver's seat and drove away. He sat there for a few minutes as Michael and the sergeant walked into the front door. When they were inside and the door closed he drove off.

Barstow drove over to Michael's house and parked within visual distance of the house. He sat there watching as a car pulled up outside of the house. When the doors opened, five women got out and went into the house. They were dressed like they were at a night club. He waited and watched for a while just to see what was going on. He could see Johnny through Michael's bedroom window looking out. He watched Johnny as he sat there with a frown on his face. He was sad that his brother had been taken from him. He noticed that Johnny turned his head quickly. He climbed down from the window and disappeared from sight.

Barstow opened the car door and got out. He leaned against the car and pulled out a pack of cigarettes. He tapped the pack and put one into his mouth. Lighting it, he stood there watching the house like a hawk. A police car pulled up to him and stopped. There were two police officers inside of the car the passenger rolled her window down,

"Good evening sir; how are you this fine evening?" she said with a joyful voice. He took a drag from his cigarette and said as he exhaled,

"Well other than the fact that I'm off duty and I'm stuck here babysitting my C.O's house, just perky." He chuckled and took another drag as she got out of the car telling the driver to stay put. She walked up to him and reached over taking the cigarette from his mouth and putting it into hers. She took a drag and asked,

"You don't remember me do you?" He looked at her trying to remember her, her face looked familiar but he couldn't remember her name. He hesitated while looking at her with a dumbfounded look. She laughed and said,

"That's ok we were both real drunk and promised each other when we exchanged numbers to stay in touch. I tried to call you but kept getting your answering machine." She took another drag and flicked the ashes then licked the butt around the edge and put it back into his mouth. She reached into her shirt pocket and pulled out a business card and placed it into his top jacket pocket. As she walked back over to the police car she turned and smiled at him seductively,

"Call me; my cell number is on the card. I meen it; for any reason what so ever." Then she got in and closed the door. He heard the other officer say as she leaned over to look at him,

"Damn, girl you ever hear of a threesome, um~, um~, um~ delicious." Then she licked her top lip as she leaned back and pulled slowly away. He pulled the card out and looked at it then put it back into his pocket.

He looked back over at the house and seen shadows on the wall of Michaels bedroom. He finished hi cigarette and started towards the house. As he walked towards the house he noticed the light come on in the bedroom where their mother sleeps. He stopped and ducked behind a tall bush. He kept his eyes on the window of her room. He san one of the women who arrived with the others standing by the window. Then he saw their mother walk up behind her and put her arms around her from behind. She leaned over and kissed the back of her neck. She moved her hands up and pushed up on her breasts as the woman looked back at her and kissed her. Barstow squinted his eyes and asked himself,

"What the hell? What kind of home did he live in?" He stood there as the boy's mother slipped the other woman's top off of her. She reached around as their mother stood behind her and undid her braw.

Barstow stepped out from behind the bush and began walking towards the house. He could see the boy's mother slowly rubbing the other woman's breasts. He thought that "if she doesn't care if anyone can see her and her friends doing that at the window, what else are they doing in that house?" He was mad yet a little turned on by seeing the two of them in the window. He didn't know what to expect when he got to the house. He didn't know if Michael's brother would be alright or if he would find him locked in a closet somewhere while they did their thing. Ether way, he knew that he had to get in and find him. Barstow's palms were sweating and he felt uneasy the closer he got to the house.

When he stepped up on the porch, he could hear the sounds of joyful screams. He checked the door to see if it was unlocked. As he turned the doorknob he noticed that the door was unlocked. He waited a few seconds before he entered the front door. As he opened the door it made a squeak so he stopped. He remembered that his father taught him to take a disposable lighter and push the button to coat the hinge to stop the squeak. He reached into his pocket and took out his lighter. He coated the hinges with the gas then put it back into his pocket. As he opened the door the squeak was no longer there. He went into the house trying not to make a sound.

When he was inside he closed the door slowly till it door cylinder latched. The sounds were even more distinct and clear to him what was going on upstairs. He walked over to the stairs and one by one he climbed each step. When he reached the top step he saw the door of her room slightly open. He quietly stepped over next to her room and looked inside trying not to be noticed. What he'd seen was a man's dream all those naked women together in one room. He had seen the two boy's mother on the bed in the middle of having sex with the woman in the window. There were five other naked women surrounding another woman who was clothed and very scared as they were trying to copse her to undress. They were fondling her and kept lifting her skirt and top as she was trying without success to make them stop. She was being held by two of them who were overpowering her. She was crying aloud for them to stop, but the more she cried the more they forced themselves on her.

Barstow was about to crash their party until he heard some noise from Michaels bedroom. He looked one last time at the women then turned and crept down the hall to Michael's room. When he got to the door he looked in and was shocked at what he'd seen. There was two women molesting Johnny as he laid there crying out for them to stop. His cries for them to stop only excited them even more, so much more they didn't notice that Barstow snuck in behind them. He was so full of rage that he put his arms around their neck and choked them until they passed out. Johnny laid there embarrassed and afraid of what Barstow was going to do.

Barstow looked over at Johnny and smiled at him,

"Don't worry son this will be our little secrete, nobody has to know what happened here. Unless you want someone to know, it's up to you son." He reached over and picked up his clothes and handed them to him. He sat down on the bed and told him that he shouldn't be ashamed of what had happened to him. Johnny put his clothes on while Barstow turned his head away from him as not to embarrass him even more than what he already was. He told him to wait here until he came back for him. When Barstow got up off of the bed, he looked at the two women with discuss and kicked them in the head as he was leaving the room.

Barstow slowly walked to the bedroom she was in with her freak friends. He stood there for a few seconds before getting close enough to see in the room. He inched closer to the slightly open door but didn't hear the sounds of panic he'd heard from the woman the who they were forcing them selves onto. When he looked into the room he saw that they had gagged her and had her bent over backwards with her top pulled over her head and her skirt and panties off. Her hands were tied away from her straight out and her legs were tied at the knees and ankles spread out as she fought to free herself. She was squirming as she was being raped by the five women. Tears were pouring out of her eyes from the savage rape as they assaulted her every way possible.

Barstow was so angry and disgusted, he seen a shotgun sitting in the closet between Johnny's bedroom and her bedroom. He picked up the gun and checked to see if it was loaded. The shotgun had two shells in it and were unused so he took a breath and kicked the door in,

"Freeze you pieces of shit!" The women all jumped from his unannounced intrusion. He pointed the gun at Michael and Johnny's mother then motioned the others over to join her at the bed. He reached down while keeping his eyes on them, picking up a sheet on the floor and covering the woman and pulling her top back down. He looked at them and told two of them to untie her,

"Get over there and untie her before I fucking kill you stupid mother fuckers!" the two of them didn't think that he would shoot them, so they leaned back and looked at him. They winked at him and one of them said as they rubbed themselves between their legs,

"You know that we can all be your fantasy, or if you want our new bitch over there can be your bitch along with us. Besides; your ex-girlfriend here told us how good you really are!" Barstow hesitated lowering the shotgun for a second and looked at her. He was the one holding them at bay and knew from his military training that the enemy will try anything to regain their freedom. He knew what they were trying to do and wasn't stupid. He was also pissed off about Johnny's mother letting Johnny be raped and not to be concerned about anyone but her. He pointed the gun at them and said,

"You heard what the fuck I said, get over there and untie her, and don't even think about touching her private parts." They were angered by his rejection and pouted as they did what he told them to do.

When they went over and freed her, she slipped off of the ottoman and chair they had her tied to. She was crying and held her groin from the pain of them raping her in her rectum with a night stick lying on the floor next to her. She angrily looked over at the women and got up grabbing the night stick and attacked them with it. Barstow stood back and let her beat the women with the night stick. He kept the shotgun trained on them while they were being beat by her. When she'd gotten her frustrations out and the five were beaten to a pulp, Barstow helped her by handing her, her clothes. She was embarrassed from the rape and started crying that Barstow was in the room. She said in a broken voice as she put her clothes on,

"I ah; I thought being raped by a man was bad, but a woman, a woman raping a woman." Barstow put his hand out and asked her,

"Do you; miss can I give you a ride home?" she slammed her fists down on the floor then put her palms to her eyes. Crying profusely she said over and over,

"Why me; why the hell me; I mean I never did anything to anybody so why did they do this to me?" she sat there on the floor pulling her knees to her chest. Johnny's mother looked over at Barstow and sarcastically said,

"Ah- you little baby; what's the matter, can't take a little adult action in an adult world? Besides I probably screwed your mother and your aunts and maybe you father too." Barstow walked over and back handed her hard enough she slammed up against the wall next to the bed. Her partner who was lying on the bed screamed as he hit her lover. He looked at her and said,

"Shut the hell up; I haven't hit you yet bitch." She rolled off of the bed and went over to consol her from being hit by Barstow. She was afraid of Barstow and thought that he was going to hit her too.

Barstow went back over to the woman and kneeled down in front of her,

"Miss; miss; what's your name? I don't know your name; what do I call you?" she looked up at Barstow with tear filled eyes and smiled at him. Barstow reached into his pocket and pulled out his handkerchief and handed it to her. She dried her eyes then blew her nose coughing from the gag they put in her mouth. She reached up and put her hand on his arm and in a timed voice she smiled and said,

"Sandy; you asked me my name; it's Sandy that's my name." Barstow smiled back at her and stood up. He reached down and helped her to her feet. He was feeling feelings of which he'd no felt before. When he looked at her he felt as if he'd rescued a damsel in distress. The way she looked at him made him feel tingly and warm all over. Barstow took his phone out of his pocket and the card out of his top jacket pocket and dialed his friend's number. When she answered he said,

"Remember when you said if I ever need anything; well I think I need you and about a dozen police officers at 2770 Fielding Lane." He looked at her and watched as she sat down on the chair. She leaned over onto the side of her hip because she couldn't sit directly on her rear due to the pain she was feeling. He stood there feeling empathy for her yet felt like he owed her something, but didn't know what it was. She knew that he had rescued her for a reason and felt as if she owed him her life.

They waited in the bedroom until the police showed up. When they arrived they saw about a dozen police cars pull up in front of the house. He walked over to the window and yelled out

"Up here; we're up here; hurry." The officers bolted into the house and up the stairs. The female officer led the group of police officers in the house and up the stairs to the room. When they came into the room, they were astonished by what they'd discovered. They saw Barstow holding a shotgun and pulled out their pistols. When they pointed their pistols at him Sandy yelled out,

"No; no; not him don't arrest him; arrest them. They fucking raped me." She started crying again,

"They picked me up while I was on my way home and asked me if I needed a ride. They brought me here with a hood over my head then left me here. Then they came back and raped me." All of the police officers were stunned by her statement. Johnny was standing in the doorway of his brother's room looking at all of the police officers. He looked scared that so many police were in his mother's bedroom. He didn't know what to think,

"Excuse me; excuse me." He said to one of them. The officer turned and looked at him. He kneeled down with one knee on the floor,

"Its ok son; everything's alright young man." He rubbed his eyes and gave him the strangest look. He looked back into his brother's room then back at the officer,

"What about them?" as he pointed into the bedroom. The officer got up and tapped on another officer's shoulder and motioned for him to look in the hall. A female officer noticed what was going on and motioned two other officers to come with her. Barstow said,

"Oh yea; there's something else; in the other bedroom there's two child molesters lying on the floor. Alive but they should be dead as far as I'm concerned." The officers who were standing by the door walked out of the bedroom and to the other bedroom where Johnny was standing. Johnny's mother spoke up,

"I didn't have anything to do with that; I wasn't in there; they did that all on their own." The officers shook their head and felt disgusted that she claimed not to know that he was being molested. They wondered that the scene of all the naked women and Sandy's condition, how she could not know. She tried to get out of the bedroom but was stopped by one of the officers. Her lover was so scared, that she urinated all over the floor where she was sitting. Johnny's mother was fighting with the officers and screaming out,

"Johnny; Johnny; don't talk to them their bad men; don't tell them anything; mommy loves you." One of the female officers punched her right in the face,

"Listen up you bitch; incase you don't see too clear; me and another officer here are women. Probably; no more of a woman than you'll ever be." She held her jaw where she'd gotten hit. She looked at her and sat down on the bed. Sandy laughed at her and looked at her with a look that could kill,

"Believe me bitch; if it is my only goal in life; you'll go to prison for the rest of your life. Along with all of these cockles men; and oh; by the way; I'll take your everything away from you. How do you like that; well bitch got your tong?" She looked at her then up at Barstow who was smiling at her then winked.

The police officers who were standing in the room chuckled and smiled when she was put in her place. The others who had went out into the hall, walked down the hall and into Michael's bedroom. When they entered they saw the other women lying on the floor. One of the officers got a good look at the women and sat down on the bed with his hands on his forehead. As he sat there he was asked by another officer,

"What's the matter; you look like something's wrong?" He just sat there looking over at the two women on the floor. The one officer kneeled down and checked their pulse. He looked at their naked bodies; the other officer smacked him with his hat,

"What the hell man; don't you know who these two women are?" The officer got up and looked at him like he was crazy. He looked down at them then back at him,

"No; no I don't know who they are; all I know is that they're a couple of female perverts who's going to jail." the officer sitting on the bed got up and grabbed his shoulders,

"These are the Mayors daughters; we just can't arrest them unless you want to guard the city dump your whole career." He looked down at them then back at him,

"Well– I guess you're right; girls this pretty and so– well built; I mean so well connected would do better in my; I mean at home with daddy wouldn't they." He patted him on the shoulders and said,

"That's right son; you made the right choice." They went back to the others and leaned over to whisper what they'd found in the other room. The two officers who'd found the two women stayed there while the two female and two male officers went to the other room to see for their selves. They were shocked to see that it was the daughters of the mayor. One of them woke up and was startled by the police standing there. One of the female officers looked at them and said,

"Well; well; well; everyone knows the two of you go to gay bars; but gay bars and children; you're despicable." She looked at the female police officer who spoke to her and smiled giving her a wink. She shook her sister to wake her up. When her sister woke up she looked at her then noticed the police. The sister who awoke first looked at her sister then at the police officer,

"If you don't arrest us we'll have sex with every police officer on the force; all at once; or do you prefer one on one action?" She looked at her with discuss and turned away from them. She pulled out her handcuffs and turned back to her. She walked over to her and smacked her as hard as she could. Then she reached down and grabbed her by the hair pulling her up off the floor,

"Put your hands behind your back." She turned her around and leaned forwards putting her cheek to her head behind her ear and told her,

"If I were you; I'd get a lawyer as slimy as you are; and oh; by the way get use to being the only child; because I'm very close to the judge; she's my lover." She closed her eyes because she knew that daddy wasn't going to get her out of this one this time. Her sister seen the way she was helped up and got up without any help from the officer. The officer reached over and her fellow female police officer handed her the handcuffs from her belt. Sense she got up without assistance from her; she gently placed the handcuffs on her. The other sister looked over at her and just to infuriate her she asked,

"What; you don't want to frisk this tasty body?" That was something she really shouldn't have said to her. The look on her face was that of death coming at you. She pulled out her pistol and put it to her forehead. She pulled the trigger, all you could hear was a "click" from the hammer hitting an empty chamber. It scared her so bad that she peed herself. The urine flowed down her legs like rivers into puddles at her feet. She started yelling and screaming at the officer as she walked away from her. She knew she'd gotten her point across by her reaction. She was smiling and a little snicker also slipped out.

She walked into the bathroom and picked up a bucket sitting next to the toilet. She turned on the cold water and filled the bucket. Then she turned off the water, lifting the bucket out of the sink, she heard her still screaming at the top of her lungs. She walked back into Michael's bedroom and threw it on her. It must have worked because she shut her mouth. The officer looked at the other officers and told them,

"Put them in the back of my car; I'll personally deliver them to the station my self." The officers took them down the stairs and outside placing them in her car. Her partner another female officer looked at her and told her to have the other officers place everyone except for Barstow and Sandy under arrest. Her partner walked over to one of the officers and told them,

"Sergeant Parks wants you to place all except Barstow and miss Sandy under arrest; charge them all with sexual misconduct with a minor, rape, felony kidnapping and any thing else you can think of; mister Barstow can you and miss Sandy take care of Johnny until we can find a suitable home for him?" Barstow looked at Sandy as the officers woke the women up Sandy knocked out earlier. They were placing handcuffs on them and standing them up. They were all confused about what had happened to them. Johnny's mother was trying to fend off the police but wasn't too successful. They slapped the cuffs on her after tackling her to the bed. After Johnny's mother had been handcuffed the female officer left to join her partner who was already in the car.

Barstow looked at Sandy and shrugged his shoulders,

"Well you did say that you wanted to take her kids from her; I guess that this is the perfect way to test your ability to take care of kids." Johnny's mother on her way out of the bedroom door along with the other women, stopped and looked her in the face,

"You may think that this is over; but it's not. It's long from over; bank on it; you will be sorry; you better look over your shoulder forever." She looked at her with her head sinking down into her shoulders. She'd scared her that bad. Barstow put his arm around her and squeezed to let her know he was there to protect her. The officer shoved her threw the door and led her down the stares to join the others who were put into the back of the paddy wagon outside. Barstow walked over to the window and watched as the female officer got into the car with her partner then they drove away. Then a few minutes later Johnny's mother emerged from the house forced by the police into the back of the paddy wagon.

Johnny was standing in the hall crying about his mother and the others being arrested. He was so scared that he had urinated on himself. Sandy heard him crying and walked out into the hall. She had a soft spot in her heart for hurt children. And to see him crying broke her heart. Barstow walked out into the hall and stood there looking at Johnny. He felt as if he'd lied to Johnny by calling the police on his mother and the other women. And at the same time, he felt as if he'd done the right thing by protecting both him and Sandy from those women who were hurting them. Sandy kneeled down and reached out for him. Johnny ran over and threw his arms around her squeezing her as he cried. Barstow looked down at the floor still feeling guilty about the police arresting Johnny's mother. Johnny looked up at Barstow,

"Thank you mister; thank you for stopping those girls from hurting me again." Barstow started tearing up and tried to hold it in but couldn't. The words that

Johnny said to him got to him unlike anyone else, coming from a child he couldn't help but to tear up. He knew that he'd made the right choice now more than before. Sandy leaned back and looked at Johnny asking him,

"How long have those girls been coming here; hurting you Johnny?" with concern in her voice. He looked at her and then at the floor,

"For a long time; maybe this long." He held up five fingers and looked at her. She asked him with a hard to believe look on her face and a shattered voice,

"How a; how old are you Johnny?" He looked at her and held up seven fingers. She bowed her head to keep Johnny from seeing the pain she was feeling. Barstow felt the same pain and anger she was feeling but kept his composure. He turned and walked down the stairs clinching his fists in anger. He walked outside and stood there trying to hold in his rage, but the rage had been unleashed on a car window. The same car that he'd seen the women pull up in earlier. The window popped like a balloon when he hit it with everything he had in him.

After he'd destroyed the window, he walked back into the house. Sandy and Johnny had already came down the stairs and seen Barstow walk in bleeding from his hand. Sandy ran into the kitchen and grabbed a dish towel. She ran back into the living room and wrapped Barstow's hand with the towel.

Johnny walked over to Barstow and touched his hand. He looked at Barstow and asked him,

"You made yourself bleed; why did you make yourself bleed?" he looked at him and smiled. Barstow kneeled down and told him,

"Son; sometimes adults do some stupid things; things that they regret later. I did something that I shouldn't have done; and I can't take it back." Johnny looked at Barstow and tried to understand what he was saying to him. He was holding his hand then leaned forwards to give him a hug,

"Do not worry; things that seem bad always turn out better in the end; you'll see." Then he backed away and Barstow stood up and asked Sandy,

"Do you think?" she interrupted saying,

"You don't have to ask; sure I'll take care of him. He'll be like my little brother; we'll have lots of fun together. Go on go do what you have to do." Barstow smiled and walked over giving her a kiss on the cheek he turned and ran out of the house. Sandy and Johnny walked over to the door and watched as Barstow ran over to his car and got in and drove away. Sandy looked down at Johnny,

"What do you think sport; up for some old people and some ice cream?" Johnny looked up at her and smiled shaking his head yes. She smiled back at him,

"Well alright then sir shall we be on our way; by the way, do you know how to drive?" Johnny laughed,

"I'm only seven." She smiled,

"Yea; me nether, guess we'll walk." Sandy and Johnny walked down the street hand in hand, singing and laughing trying not to think about what they'd just been through.

CHAPTER

2

The two police officer's were driving towards the station when sergeant Parks made a turn on to an old logging road. The road hasn't been used in over twenty years and was full of potholes. Sergeant Parks looked in the rearview mirror at the two sisters every time she hit a pothole. She watched as their breasts jiggled from the jolt of the potholes. Sergeant Parks partner asked,

"Why are we going to the old logging camp?" she smiled and looked over at her. She hesitated for a couple of seconds then licked her lips,

"I have a little something to show you that I know you're going to love." She was nervous and felt as if her sergeant was up to something she didn't think she wanted to be a part of. Sergeant Parks was just about at the camp when she pulled up to a gate. She stopped the car and took a key off of her clip on her belt and handed it to Officer Malone. She looked at sergeant parks and got out of the car. Officer Malone walked over to the gate and unlocked it. As she pushed the heavy gate, Parks looked back at the two sisters and winked at them.

The oldest sister slid down in the seat and spread her legs apart. Sergeant Parks reached back as she kept her eyes on Malone who was having a difficult time opening the gate. She reached over to the older sister and started rubbing her inner thy. She slowly moved her hand closer to her vagina. Sergeant parks looked back at Malone and seen she had the gate open and pulled her hand back as she turned around. The older sister sat back up and looked at her sister as she leaned over to her and whispered,

"Sergeant Parks is a man." The younger sister looked at her and felt nervous because her and her sister was nude and handcuffed in the back seat. Her sister knew about her being raped as a little girl and the police never caught the rapist. She began to cry and was fearful of what she thinks that Parks has in mind. Her older sister whispered,

"Calm down sis; don't let on that you know Parks is a man." Malone walked back over to the car and got in. She told Parks,

"Alright; the gates open now what?" Parks drove up to the camp and pulled up in front of the bunk house. Parks put the car in park and opened the door. He told Malone,

"Come on; we'll check out the building then come back for the girls." Malone looked back at the girls and saw that the youngest sister was upset but kept quiet as she followed orders from her sergeant. She wanted to say something but felt that would be a career killer. Her and Parks got out of the car and walked toward the building. Parks went into the building first and was followed a few seconds later by Malone.

Malone felt someone grab her and slammed her up against the wall inside of the building. She was forced to her knees as she felt her hands being pulled up and handcuffs put on her wrists. Tears trickled from her eyes as the pain of being manhandled was excruciating. She pleaded with whomever it was to stop as she hoped that sergeant Parks would rescue her from her attacker but help never came. She felt someone reach around and rip her shirt and grasp her breasts. She begged for her attacker to stop; but it only made it worst. She was forced up from the floor by her gun belt and pushed tightly against the wall.

Parks leaned over and in his normal voice he told her,

"I've been watching you for a long time; studying you; watching until the time was right." In a panicky tone of voice she asked,

"Right; right for what?" he leaned forward and kissed her ear,

"To take you as my queen; and to bear my children." She cried more intensely and pleaded with him not to carry through with what he was planning to do. She started panicking and kept saying,

"Parks; Parks; help me; please help me." But she didn't know that Parks was the one who was doing this to her because it was too dark for her to see. He reached around and unbuckled her gun belt throwing it away from her. He picked her up and carried her over to the bed and put her on it face down. He turned her over enough to unbutton her pants. He pulled her off her boots then her pants and panties. The only thing she had on was her braw and ripped shirt. She felt a knife against her skin as he cut her braw exposing her rather large breasts. Then he cut the sleeves of her shirt and pulled it off of her. He rolled her back over face down on the bed and climbed on top of her. She begged him not to do this but he enjoyed her pleas for him to stop. Her pleas only excited him even more.

A few minutes of begging satisfied his need for the time being so he climbed off of her and told her,

"Woman; if you attempt to get up and leave this place; my soldiers shall kill you." She was so scared that she would die she turned her head and continued to weep as he left her and went outside. He walked over to the car and opened the back door. One by one he pulled the two girls from the car and held on to the handcuffs so they couldn't escape.

He let go of the handcuffs and reached down and squeezed their firm buttocks and said to them,

"Well; well young ladies you're in for a special treat. Oh yes; I forgot to tell you; scream all you want nobody will hear you." They started begging him not to do this, but he ignored their pleas for release as he laughed at them begging like little children. He was on top of the world and was enjoying every bit of making them feel degraded as women. As they walked toward the bunkhouse he stopped and held the oldest sister's handcuffs while he stepped behind her sister and forced her to hold his penis in her hands. He leaned over and asked her,

"Feel like old times doesn't it; just like when I took you from your bedroom when you were of breading age." Her sister started crying because she now knows who it is that raped her little sister when she was thirteen. She tried to pull away from him but he grabbed her by the hair and pulled her back and told her,

"You are mine to do with what he desire; and I desire you your older sister and Malone to breed with me." He pulled up on her hair to get her to stand up then held on to her handcuffs as he led them into the bunkhouse. When he opened the door he pushed them into the room. They fell to the floor as he closed the door and locked it. He walked over to the fireplace and snapped his fingers. The fireplace ignited illuminating the room. They saw Malone on the bed naked and her clothes on the floor scattered about the floor. He walked over and pulled up on their handcuffs forcing them to their feet. He walked them over to the bed and forced them to lay face down on the bed with Malone.

He climbed up on the bed and one by one he pulled them to him. As they were held down he spread their legs apart and penetrated them until he expelled bodily fluids into each of them. He was so forceful and overpowering that by the time he'd finished with them, they lay exhausted and near death. He removed the handcuffs from them and waited for a few minutes. He smiled and told each one of them,

"By the power of Lucifer you have all three conceived and shall bear six children each." All they could do was to lay there and hope that he didn't kill them. Malone tried to muster enough strength to ask the oldest sister to forgive her for being a part of bringing her and her sister to this hell hole. She smiled at her with what little strength she had left,

"Don't blame yourself for what happened to us; our desire got us into this predicament." She smiled and kissed her on the lips and winked at her. She slowly turned to her sister and checked to see if she was alright. She was so exhausted she passed out from the rape by Parks. She looked back at Malone and told her that Parks was the one who'd raped her sister when she was only thirteen. Malone closed her eyes and said,

"I'm so sorry; I had no idea that Parks was a rapist. I didn't even know that he was a man; nether did anyone else." She smile at Malone and asked her in a stutter,

"When and if we get out of this; do you think; I mean I've seen you at the bars my sister and I go to." She smiled and said to her,

"The three of us move in together? It would be my pleasure to have the two of you living with me." The older sister smiled at her and fell off to sleep. A few seconds later Malone also fell of to sleep.

While they slept, Parks took the handcuffs off of them and dressed each of them in a see through white full length gown. He placed each of them on a pentagram he'd drawn on the floor in front of the fireplace. He had also injected them with a hallucinogenic then left them to run a few errands. When he left Malone awoke and looked over at the sisters then noticed the pentagram they were all on. She slid across the floor to reach the others who were just a few feet away. The first of the two sisters she'd reached was the youngest. She shook her until she awoke and seen her over top of her.

Still groggy from the drug Parks injected her with; she smiled and said in a timid voice,

"Where are we?"

"We're still at the old logging camp." Then Malone brushed back the hair from her face and smiled at her. She looked up at her and then around the room. She tried to get up but the drug had taken effect on her and she felt glued to the floor. Malone was able to stand up because the dosage was a lot smaller than what she done when she was younger. Because of that she was able to function with little restriction. She looked around for her weapon; but it seems that Parks had hidden her weapon where she couldn't find it. She staggered around the room and found an old leather bound book with a pentagram etched on the front cover.

She picked up the book and sat down on the bed. She opened it and seen a picture of Parks drawn on one of the pages. On the same page the inscription was what looked like a spell to her; or some kind of chant. She looked a few pages further and seen what looked like the three of them to a tee. She put her hand over her mouth as do all women when they see something that scares them. She closed the book and felt some of the floor boards were loose; so she lifted the floor boards and put the book down in the floor and replaced the floor board. She put a chest over the floor boards so he wouldn't notice that she had put the book in the floor.

By then the older sister awoke and slowly got up from the floor. Her head was woozy from the drug but was able to get up and move about. Malone went over and helped her to regain her balance. But the drug was not a strong as he thought it would be and they both helped her sister to her feet. The oldest sister looked at Malone and told her,

"You still don't know our names do you?" she looked at her,

"I was going to get around to that before the two of you move in with me; honestly I was; but for now we've got to get way from here." They both put the younger sister's arm over their shoulder and left the old bunkhouse. They made their way into the woods a few hundred yards away.

About three hours has passed from the time they left the logging camp. Malone spotted the lights from the town and stopped for them to rest. They sat the youngest sister down on the ground up against a tree. She was awake and suffering from the effects of the drug she'd been injected with. She thought that she'd seen angels following them the whole way from the camp. When she told her sister she'd seen their grandparents following them the whole time, she took it as she was hallucinating from the drugs. She'd also told her that there were a bunch of people standing around them looking out for Parks,

"Pinkie; grandma and grandpa are standing behind you and they have a lot of friend with them." Pinkie looked over at her sister and told her that was impossible; because they'd been dead for twelve years now,

"Linda; you know that's impossible; our grandparents are in heaven with all of their family; our family." She looked over at Pinkie and Malone with a dazed look on her face and started singing a song she hasn't herd sense they were kids going to church. It was a song that their grandparents loved to hear them sing together in front of the congregation. She seemed to be speaking to someone and someone speaking back to her. She said something that made her believe that in fact she was speaking with her deceased grandparents. She spoke about the ring that her grandmother gave Pinkie that belonged to her great grandmother. Linda had no idea that the ring was given to Pinkie; because it had been a secrete between Pinkie and her grandmother that Linda knew nothing about.

Linda told them about a war that has been taking place for centuries between Heaven and Hell and was about to involve mankind. She seemed to be very sure of what she was saying,

"Grandma; what do you mean that a war like we've never seen before? I don't understand what this has to do with us." She started to cry and her voice changed with a cry in it.

"Who's that over there grandpa? That man over there with the wavy hair and beard; and why does he have holes in his hands and feet?" she started smiling and told Pinkie and Malone that they have to get to the old church just outside of L.A. She also told them that Private Barstow and Michael Talon must go with them. Malone knew where Barstow and Talon were; and she would take them to the both of them.

Malone and Pinkie helped Linda up and they made their way toward the town. They walked through the woods until they came to Malone's house. She told them to come inside while she got some things together for the trip to L.A. When she went into the bathroom she had to go pee. As she started to urinate she felt a deep burning sensation coming from her urethra. It was so intense that she thought she was burning in a fire. She screamed out in pain from the burning sensation. Pinkie ran into the bathroom when she herd her screaming,

"What's wrong; are you alright?" She was sitting there; splashing water from the sink on herself trying to stop the burning. She spread her legs open as far as she could to try and cool down. Pinkie looked in horror as she saw blood seeping from around her vaginal area. She ran into the kitchen and emptied the ice trays into a large bowel. She looked over at the counter and saw a box of zip lock bags she grabbed one of them and filled it with the ice. She ran back into the bathroom and took out the bag of ice and placed it on her vagina. She told her to hold it there until the burning stopped. Malone looked up and smiled at her; thanking her for helping.

Pinkie herd Linda screaming out in the living room; screaming,

"Help; help me; it hurts; make it stop; make it stop." Pinkie ran out to see what was wrong with her sister. She saw her sitting on the floor holding her self between her legs. There was blood in a pool on the floor under her. She went over and helped her from the floor and into the bath room. Pinkie put her sister into the tube and turned on the cold water. She put the stopper into the drain and looked at Malone,

"What the hell is going on?" about that time she also started to feel a burning feeling as well. It was even more intense for her because she had started her monthly cycle. She doubled over in pain; she was hurting so bad she fell to the floor. Malone got up and helped her up. She helped her over to the tube and she got in with her sister. Her sister looked up at Malone with a dazed look on her face,

"They told me to have you go get Barstow and bring him here to us. He will know what to do." She looked at Pinkie and had a tear in her eye. With a chocked up voice she leaned over and told her,

"I'll be back as soon as I can." She kissed her on the top of her head then leaned over to Linda and did the same to her. She left the bath room turned back and looked at them and took a deep breath. She turned and walked out grabbing the keys for her car off of the table next to the door. She heard Pinkie moaning from the pain she was in. That sent shivers down her spine. She locked the door and closed it as she left to get Barstow and bring him back too her house.

As she got into her car she saw a group of wild dogs sitting just down the street. It was if they were watching her as she left to get Barstow. She sat there for a few minutes to see if they would leave; but they stayed there not budging from where they were. She opened her glove box and pulled out a nine millimeter pistol.

She checked the clip for rounds and took the safety off. As she started the car they got up and moved; making a path for her to leave. She slowly pulled out of her driveway and started down the street. As she passed them; it looked as if they bowed to her. One of them even looked as if it was trying to speak to her. Two of them started to follow her as she drove on and the others stayed there watching the house.

The ones that stayed started howling then moved towards the house. They walked up onto the front porch and started scratching at the door. They were trying to get into the house where Pinkie and Linda were. They heard them trying to get in and grew very frightened of them. They were so afraid; they hugged each other for comfort. Linda let loose her arms from her sister and told her,

"Do not fear my sister; for they are forbidden to enter. We are safe." Pinkie let her go and looked at her and regained her composer as the scratching stopped and the dogs went away.

CHAPTER

3

As Malone drove through town; she didn't see anyone on the street. The whole town was dark; no street lights, traffic signals, not even one single house light were on. She drove by the station house and even that was dark. She knew that something had happened, and the fear she felt grew a lot stronger. When she passed the old cemetery, she noticed that the gates looked as if they were ripped from their hinges. She stopped the car and started to get out; that's when she looked in her rearview mirror. The dogs that were following her were joined by too many other dogs for her to count.

Malone reached into the back seat and grabbed the duffel bag her friend from the FBI gave her. She opened it and took out the cell phone sitting in the top. When she turned it on, the dogs charged at her car. The attack was vicious and scared her more than she'd ever been scared before. The sound of the cell phone must have been heard by the dogs which made them attack her. She reached back into the bag and pulled out a mini machine gun and thirty or forty clips. There was a flare gun and shells at the bottom of the bag.

She pulled out the gun and loaded it with one of the shells. Reaching up she rolled her sunroof open just enough that she pointed the gun and fired off a round. The flair exploded above the car which scared the dogs enough that they stopped their attack. The dog retreated and regrouped behind her car fifty or sixty yards away. She opened the cell phone and found her friends number. She highlighted it and pushed the send button. While the phone was dialing, a car came out from nowhere. It was traveling fast towards her. Just before it would have ran into her, it turned and headed straight for the dogs. The car plowed into the dogs and circled back.

As the phone was ringing the driver held up his phone which was lit up. He answered it,

"Hello; you rang?" she was upset and had a shattered tone in her voice as she spoke.

"Hello Gabriel is; is that you?" she was crying and put the cell phone in her lap as she laid her head against the steering wheel. He beeped his horn at her and turned on his interior light. She lifted her head and put the phone up to her ear,

"I don't understand; how did you get here so fast?" he smiled and told her,

"Don't worry about that right now; the main thing is to get where Linda told you to go; and do what she told you to do." As he spoke she could see him start to glow with a bluish white tint. She started to smile and shook her head yes. She started to get the idea that someone was watching out for her and wanted her to succeed in getting her where she needed to go. Gabriel put his car in drive and waited for her to lead the way to the Academy. She looked in her rear view and seen the dogs that had escaped being hit regrouped and charged after them. She put her car in drive and took off with Gabriel close behind her.

As they drove on the lights from the street lamps came on one by one as they passed them. She looked in her rear view and seen Gabriel put his hand out of his window and snap his fingers. As if a light switch had been turned on; the whole town one by one; the lights came on. But the dogs even though they were a ways behind them kept following; joined by even more dog than before. By the time they'd reached the Academy, there must have been close to fifty dogs chasing them.

The guard at the gate saw the cars heading towards him and stepped out in front of them thinking he could make them stop. Malone and Gabriel didn't slow down but instead sped up and caused the guard to jump out of the way. They crashed through the gate arm and drove straight for the main building. The guard managed to get to his feet and called the security office sounding the alarm. He seen all of the dogs chasing them and turned around when he noticed that there were four of them standing behind him growling at him. Before he could close the door of the guard shack; he was attacked by the dogs. He did everything he could to defend himself, but they overpowered him.

Gabriel felt the death of the guard and wept. But he knew that he had to keep going and let nothing stand in the way of what must happen. They pulled up in front of the main building and were met by a half of a dozen armed soldiers. They threw the cars into park a jumped out. The dogs were half way up the front lawn charging at full speed. Malone and Gabriel aimed and opened fire on the dogs. The soldiers began firing at the dogs; as Malone and Gabriel made a break for the front door. The soldiers one by one turned and ran for the door. One of the soldiers had got bitten by a rather large dog. As it griped a hold of his pant leg, he aimed at it and pulled the trigger. As the dog lay lifeless on the ground, he ran for the door.

The others kept firing at the rest of the dogs. There was what seemed like more dogs outside than when they first arrived. Still they kept firing until everyone was safe inside. The Commandant had been standing between the fireplace and bookcase. He was so scared and was trying hard to become part of the wall. He was saying over and over,

"No; no; not again; not again." He started weeping like a child. He dropped the poker on the floor in front of him. Gabriel walked over to him and stood there for a second in front of him. He reached out and placed his hand on the Commandants shoulder. Gabriel's hand started to glow and he looked up at Gabriel. The Commandants tears turned to a smile. He felt a feeling that he'd never felt before; it was a feeling of peace and contentment. Gabriel said,

"Fear not child; for what you fear is that of fear from you past. If you truly wish to fear no longer; you have the power to change your true path." He shook his head and kneeled down in front of Gabriel and bowed his head,

"Thank you; I see now." He slowly stood up as Gabriel stood in front of him. He walked over to the window facing the front yard. As he looked out of the window; there were what looked to be hundreds of them. Dogs of all shapes and sizes, all breads with one thing in common; they were trying to get in. He didn't know why they were trying so hard to get in; but it wasn't going to happen on his watch. He walked over to the reception desk and picked up the microphone. He flipped the power button to the on position and tested it to see if it was working. When he heard the click coming through the speaker; he held the microphone to his mouth,

"Attention; Attention; all personnel and students to the main entrance immediately; we are under attack; this is not a drill. I repeat; we are under attack; this is not a drill." The room started to fill up with soldiers and students. Most of which were dressed in their bed attire. Barstow and Michael were with some of the last of the students to arrive. Gabriel looked over at Michael and smiled. He walked over and kneeled down in front of him.

Michael stepped back from him; and Barstow put his hand on Gabriel's shoulder. Barstow who was concerned with the reaction Michael had to the stranger squeezed his shoulder. Gabriel spoke up,

"Fear not my actions; for I have traveled great distances to find and serve you my Lord. I have been sent to help to protect you on your journey to your destiny my Lord." Barstow let his grasp loosen and stepped in front of Michael facing Gabriel. Until he knows his intentions, he wasn't going to let Gabriel near him. Gabriel started to reach into his inside jacket pocket, but was stopped by Barstow. He grabbed Gabriel's wrist and his pistol at the same time; aiming it at him. Gabriel smiled and said,

"Still the cautious man; still making sure before you make your move." Barstow looked at him and wondered what he was talking about. Michael tugged on Barstow's shirt tail. Barstow turned his head to look at Michael. Michael looked over at Gabriel then back up at Barstow,

"It's ok; I trust him." Michael moved over to him and smiled.

"I know you don't I; and just how is it I know you?" Gabriel bowed his head and paused for a moment,

"It is written that the five shall journey to a sacred place of worship; one that had been long forgotten. The five; three who had been tainted by evil; one who shall be the protector; and a boy who shall be trained and taught the path of the light." Michael had the strangest look on his face when he told him of the five. Barstow had let Gabriel go and stood there as he pulled out an old necklace from his jacket pocket. He told Michael that the necklace was for him to wear for protection from evil. Gabriel stood up and turned to Barstow; bowing his head and turning towards the Commandant.

He walked over to him and told him to deploy his people where he may. The Commandant reached up to a book on the bookcase; of course it was war and peace his favorite. He pulled the book half way and stepped back away from the bookcase. It slid open; what was behind it shocked everyone. He had an arsenal stashed behind the bookcase. Every weapon you could imagine was there; even armor from way back in World War One was stored there. He had everyone enter the armory and told Barstow to turn on the switches on the wall next to the door. When Barstow flipped on the switches; one by one the florescent lights over head turned on. The lights revealed not only army equipment; but Naval and Air force as well.

The massive amounts of military hardware was too much for them to take in. He asked,

"So? Do you think maybe we have a chance to beat this thing that's after one of my soldiers? Or do you think that maybe I have to put in a call for more equipment?" Gabriel smiled and looked at the Commandant,

"No child; this could come in pretty much handy for what you must do." The Commandant told the staff to issue weapons and ammo to all of the senior and junior class's. Then he ordered them to take up positions at high points of defense of Head Quarters. One by one the students drew weapons and ammo from the arsenal and went up to the upper floors and the roof top. They took up positions and awaited orders while the others were given the task of supply for the upper classmen. The Commandant put his hand on Michael's shoulder as Michael looked on with anticipation. He told him,

"Hold on there young man; you have a duty not to this institute; but to something much greater. You must fulfill this duty and act upon it as a soldier in need of a fight; no matter how long it takes you; you will be victorious." He snapped to attention and saluted Michael with pride. Michael snapped to attention and saluted him back,

"Carry on Commandant; fight well; win well; and take no prisoners." The Commandant pointed to an armored troop carrier and told them that was their ride to their destination. Michael smiled at the commandant and the Commandant smiled back at him as they ran over to the carrier. Michael was the last one into the carrier. Looking back at the Commandant; he saw him in his glory. The old war horse was at war again with his courage at maximum. Michael quietly said to himself,

"Fight well my Commandant; fight well." Then he climbed inside of the troop carrier.

Barstow was at the machine gunners post while Malone manned the driver's seat. She started up the engine and pulled out of the belly of the Academy. Heading for her house; Gabriel ask her,

"Do you know where you're going?" she looked at him and back at the road in front of her. She was worried about Pinkie and Linda because she'd been away for too long. She just kept driving and thinking that she didn't know who or what Parks really was. She was angrier at herself than at anyone else; because she had been fooled by him. And he'd seen her naked in the shower doing personal things to her self that were personal. And this she regrets more than anything in the world. Off in the distance they hear gun fire coming from the Academy. The sound grew fainter the further they got from them. Barstow looked much to his surprise; a small group of dogs started chasing the troop carrier. He pulled back on the bolt and the sound of a round loaded into the chamber. He wanted to save ammo; so he set the machine gun on Simi Automatic and took it off of safety. He took aim and squeezed off a round; hitting one of the dogs in the chest. The caliber of ammo entered its chest dime size and exited its rectum soccer ball size. He squeezed off another round then another and then one more; killing the other dogs with just as much grotesque results as the first dog.

Malone entered the street she lived on and seen no dogs anywhere in sight. She drove up to her house and put the troop carrier into park. She started to get out of her seat when Gabriel grabbed her by the arm. She struggled to break free; but his grip was over powering. He looked as if he'd seen a ghost as he looked at her. Barstow spotted something at the end of the street and turned the machine gun towards it turning on the spotlight. Gabriel said,

"Balentar!" then sat there with a stern look on his face. Balentar slowly walked towards them,

"Gabriel; guardian of the gates of Heaven; and Michael; as a child; oh how quaint." He stopped and laughed while they sat in the troop carrier. Malone looked at Gabriel,

"Are you shitting me? The guardian of the gates of Heaven; are you fucking shitting me?" she had a look of someone who'd been lied to on her face. Michael was sitting there; shaking like a leaf. Gabriel looked at Michael,

"Be calm Michael; it is not your time yet; he can not harm you; you have the amulet of God around your neck." Michael shook his head yes as he started to calm down. Barstow fired off a round at Balentar; hitting him square in the forehead but it didn't affect him at all. He looked and couldn't figure out why he was still standing when he should be dead on the ground in a pool of blood. Barstow said to himself,

"That's impossible; I know I hit him; why in the hell isn't he dead?" Balentar started laughing at Barstow. Malone knew she had to get Pinkie and Linda in to the troop carrier before Balentar could get close. Malone asked if he could cause a distraction while she went to get Pinkie and Linda from her house. Barstow said,

"No problem; get ready and move your ass as soon as you hear a big boom, boom." Gabriel let her go and she climbed out of the driver's seat and opened the rear hatch. Barstow seen she was ready and fired a round at a car near Balentar. The car exploded and Malone made a dash for the house. She went into the bath room and the two of them were sound asleep in the tub.

Malone shook them; waking them she helped them to their feet. She walked them to the front door and caught the attention of Barstow. He shook his head and aimed for another car near Balentar. He fired a round and the car exploded; giving them a chance to get out of the house and into the troop carrier. Gabriel and Michael helped them into the carrier. Once inside; Malone started up the carrier and backed away from the front of the house. Balentar laughed and said,

"Come on Gabriel; all I want is what's rightfully mine; nothing more nothing less. The book and the bitches; they are rightfully mine; fair and square. And oh by the way stupid; you can't kill something that never lived." Gabriel looked at Malone and laughed. He shook his head,

"You are really smart or totally stupid Malone; which one is it?" He put the palms of his hands over his face and leaned back in the seat.

"Do you know what the book is that he wants? Oh- man." Balentar started walking towards them as Malone put the troop carrier in drive and sped away. Barstow watched as they got further and further away from Balentar. Malone was angry that Gabriel thought that she was stupid. So angry that she wept because he thought that the book she hid was more important than her and the other two women's lives. She glanced back at Gabriel for a second and seen him laughing,

"Hey dumb ass; that's right mister high and mighty." Gabriel stopped laughing and looked at her,

"If it wasn't for people like you in this world, there wouldn't be a need for people like me to kick; their; ass." She slammed on the breaks and Gabriel fell forwards towards her. His head wound up at her thigh. She looked down and smiled,

"Night; night ass hole." She punched him so hard she knocked him out cold. The two sisters laughed along with Michael. She took her foot off of the break and stepped on the accelerator. As the carrier sped down the road Michael looked up at her and said,

"Miss Malone; do not worry about how to get where we are going. I know how to get there; my grandma told me. She'll get us there." Malone knew Michael's grandmother passed away awhile back and played along with him. She smiled and kept driving glancing back at Michael and winked at him. Michael smiled and sat back in his seat. Barstow climbed down and closed the hatch above him. He seen Gabriel laying on the floor out cold,

"Couldn't keep his mouth shut Malone?" he sat down in a seat between Michael and the oldest sister. Malone smiled and kept on driving. The two sisters started fading off to sleep the hum of the engine made it that much easier for them. Barstow put his arm around Michael and Michael laid his head against his chest. As Michael faded off to sleep he positioned his body on the empty seats and laid across Barstow's lap. Malone glanced back at Barstow,

"Good looking son you have there Barstow; looks a little like you." Barstow looked at her with a strange look on his face. He was stunned that she said what she said; he felt as if she knows more than what she's letting on. She looked at him and took a deep breath,

"I have something to tell you. But not yet; not till we are alone and the time is right." Barstow had a puzzled look on his face wondering what she was talking about. There was something about her; a feeling that he can't shake.

CHAPTER

4

As they drove through the night; the thought of what Malone said to him kept his curiosity. He kept thinking to himself,

"Did I do something wrong; did I hurt her in some way that I'm just now regretting; what did I do?" he started to say something but stopped himself before he did. She smiled and softly bit down on her lip as she thought about the past. Something he doesn't remember but she does very fondly.

A light came on and a buzzer went off on the panel. The light was yellow and said low fuel. A half a mile ahead she could see the lights from a gas station. Malone was worried that they wouldn't make it to the gas station; as low as she was on fuel. She kept her eye on the gage and hoped for the best. She reduced her speed by fifteen mile per hour to conserve fuel.

As they were pulling into the gas station; the engine sputtered. She let up off of the accelerator and coasted to the gas pump. Barstow opened the door on the back of the carrier and stepped out. The attendant walked up to him with a smile on his face,

"Don't see many of these around these parts. World War two is it?" Barstow smiled and turned to open the cap on the carrier. He took the pump handle and stuck it into the opening. The attendant stood there watching him as he pumped the gas,

"Pretty large tank is it; I mean the gas tank not the; well I can see it's no a tank. It's a people thing; you know." Barstow smiled and looked at him,

"Yea; it's a people thing; it takes people to people places; to do people things. You know." The attendant got the idea that he was being a little too nosey and walked away. He walked back to the station house and picked up the phone. He could see him smiling and waving at him as he pumped the gas. When he hung the phone up; the attendant walked back out and stood there with his hands in his pockets. He kept staring and bouncing back and forth smiling at Barstow as he pumped the gas.

Malone stepped out of the carrier and walked around to Barstow,

"Barstow; Barstow; coming up the road; there's a convoy of pick up's heading our way." Barstow took his hand off of the pump and walked to the front of the carrier to get a good look. He looked back over at the attendant, who was cackling,

"Redneck son of a bitch called them." He walked quickly over to him and the smile on his face went away. He grabbed him by the collar and jacked him up against the front of the station house. He was so mad he had spit running down from the corners of his mouth. He pleaded with Barstow not to hurt him,

"Please; please don't hurt me; there's a reward for the six of you. A million dollars each; we couldn't pass it up." Barstow threw him up against the wall and ran for the carrier yelling to Malone to get into the carrier. Malone ran into the carrier just as the convoy pulled into the gas station.

They threw their trucks into park and jumped out with shot guns and rifles just as Barstow made it into the carrier shutting the hatch behind him. Malone jumped into the driver seat and started the engine. She threw the carrier into drive and headed for them. As she got closer, they jumped for their lives just as she rammed their trucks.

She kept driving as they got to their feet and fired at them. Their guns were no match for the three inch armor plating. Michael and the two sisters awoke as did Gabriel. The gun fire sounded like firecrackers, and the bullets hitting the armor sounded like hail. The further from them they got the quieter the sounds became.

Gabriel sat up and looked at Malone,

"What was on your mind? That hurt." Malone snickered as she glanced at him while she drove. Barstow sitting beside Michael sort of chuckled a bit. Gabriel asked where they were. Malone looked at the street signs and seen a sign that said, Bolder Colorado twelve miles. She told Gabriel,

"We'll be in Bolder Colorado in about fifteen or twenty minutes; we're twelve miles east." Gabriel got up from the floor and sat across from Linda. She seen blood on his forehead and moved across sitting next to him. She reached down and ripped some of the material from the bottom of the gown she was wearing. She started dabbing the blood from his wound, trying to stop the bleeding.

As Linda was working on Gabriel, he told Malone to head to Las Angelis and he would drive as soon as she reached the city limits. Malone asked him,

"Are you sure you can handle such a beautiful woman as this one?" Gabriel let out a sarcastic snicker. Malone smiled and kept her eyes on the road ahead. Thoughts of what she needs to tell Barstow are heavy on her mind. She feels as if she's going to explode if she doesn't tell him soon before she chickens out and never lets him in on her secrete.

Malone spotted a sign ahead that said Las Angelis, but didn't pay attention to how far. She felt that something was wrong somewhere ahead of them. It was a feeling she'd felt before back home, when the towns bank was robed, and all of the hostages were executed by the bank robbers. It was a feeling that she just couldn't shake.

When they were about a mile from the California state line she noticed that a road block had been set up by the California high way patrol. She stopped and sat there watching them as they watched her. She reached up and closed the shield over the glass in front of her. She told Gabriel,

"Well; do you want to take over now; or do you want to wait until L.A. to take the wheel?" Gabriel got up and looked out of the view finder on top of the carrier. He told Malone to let him behind the wheel. Malone got up and Gabriel sat down in the driver seat and floored the accelerator. He didn't let up as he picked up speed and crashed through the cars blocking the road. The C.H.P officers jumped out of the way of the spinning cars. The finder hooked onto one of the C.H.P cars, and dragged it about three hundred feet down the road behind them. Gabriel was running about sixty miles per hour and didn't let up off of the accelerator.

When he reached L.A. he drove into some woods near the old section of the city. This was the place that the settlers first occupied and was long sense abandoned. No body goes near there anymore, because they're caught up in their modern luxuries. The only one's who've been out there, are preachers and priests to meditate.

Gabriel opened the shield to see better. Barstow and Malone opened the side covers so they could see out as they drove down through the woods on the old wagon trail. They could see the ruins of buildings long sense forgotten. Michael looked at Pinkie and shook her, but she wouldn't wake up. Malone sat down next to her and felt her pulse. Her pulse was rapped and she felt like she was on fire.

As Gabriel pulled into a clearing, they saw a large old church in the middle of the clearing. Pinkie seemed to wake up and her pulse slowed and her body temperature went back down to normal. She told them of the strangest dream she had.

"I dreamed that I was on a quest; but the quest was strange and all of you were with me." Gabriel stopped in front of the church and put the carrier into park. He got up out of his seat and looked at them,

"Stay here; I'll be back in a little while." He walked to the back of the carrier and opened the door. When he stepped down onto the ground he looked back at them and smiled. A calm feeling came over all of them as Gabriel started to glow with a soft light blue light. He looked at Michael and closed his eyes as he bowed his head; he said,

"Fear not; for you are in the presents of the one. You are safe here and shall have no harm come to you." Then he turned and walked slowly towards the Church. As he walked the glow intensified with every step.

When he reached the church, he stopped next to pillar at the door. He put his hand on the stone placard. He pressed the center stone and the doors opened. They watched as Gabriel opened the doors. He turned and walked into the open doorway, disappearing from sight.

Barstow climbed out of the carrier and walked to the front. He was joined by Malone and the two sisters. Michael got out and stood next to the back of the carrier. A small dog appeared at the edge of the clearing. For some reason the dog wouldn't come past the edge of the clearing.

Gabriel appeared at the open doorway dressed in a long snow white robe. He was joined by a man who was also dressed in a snow white robe. His hair and beard was course and also white as snow. The man stepped forward and held his arms open,

"Come forth my children; come in and join me in the safety of my humble home." The dog seemed to be nervous and started growling at the man. The dog cowered down when the stranger clapped his hands together. He walked across the clearing past Barstow and the others. He walked over to the dog and kneeled down in front of it. The dog bowed down and covered its eyes. The man reached down and picked it up and stared petting it.

"Why do you wish to harm these people? They mean you no harm; they only wish to be safe. Harm them not little one and come join us." He put the dog down and it turned to him looking as if it understood him. The dog walked over to Michael and sat down next to him. Michael reached down as the dog put its head against his leg and started petting it.

The stranger walked over to Michael and put his hand on his shoulder. Michael looked up at him and smiled. He told Michael,

"Walk with me child; and I shall tell you of the glories which await you. It is your destiny and always has been that you come here." Michael walked with him to the church. After they went inside, Gabriel motioned for the others to come inside.

Barstow and Malone walked slowly together with Linda and Pinkie to the church. As they walked up the stares, an overwhelming feeling came over them. It was a feeling which none of them have ever felt their whole life.

They walked into the church and seen an amazing sight. The church was illuminated with a brilliant golden light.

Michael and the stranger were standing next to a box in the center of the room. The stranger placed his hand on the box and the top slid open. Gabriel walked over to where Michael and the stranger were standing. He stood next to him and looked at the four of them. He smiled and looked at the stranger,

"Lord; we have come to you as in the writings of the twelve disciples had spoke about." Barstow walked over to Gabriel and held out his hand. Gabriel reached out and shook Barstow's hand,

"I am sorry for the way I've acted towards you Gabriel; would you please forgive me?" Gabriel smiled and nodded his head as he shook Barstow's hand. Michael smiled because he made his peace with Gabriel. Malone smiled and walked over to the box. Looking at Michael then at the Lord, she asked for forgiveness as she kneeled before him. Pinkie and Linda also walked over and kneeled before him asking for forgiveness.

Gabriel grasped Barstow's hand and put his arm around his back as he led him over to the Lord. Barstow stood there in front of the Lord, humbling himself and kneeling down at his feet. He looked up at the Lord and tears came to his eyes. He trembled as he asked,

"Lord; please forgive me and all of my sins; please Lord; I beg of you." He put his palm on Barstow's forehead and smiled at him. As he kneeled before him, the Lord told him,

"Arise my child and stand before me a new man. A new child as do the other three who journeyed such a long way with you." Barstow stood up slowly and felt as if he was a new person. The Lord walked over to the open box and told them to follow him as he stepped into the box.

He walked down a flight of stares as the others followed. Gabriel was the last to go down the stares behind them. Michael who was behind the Lord, watched as the Lord waved his hand in front of the door at the end of the hallway. The door opened and the Lord waited as the others to gather near him.

He turned and walked into the room, followed by the others. Inside there was three golden thrones and a beautiful golden box. He told Malone, Linda and Pinkie,

"Step forwards my children; come to me and I shall remove the evil which dwells within you. The seed which was planted within you by the evil one; I shall remove before it grows." He watched with a smile on his face as they walked to him. He looked at Malone and took her by the hand,

"Child; the book in which you found and hid is that of pure evil. It must never be removed from where you've hidden it. Do you understand? My child that book can end this world and all that my father has created." Malone nodded her head that she understood. He smiled and walked over to a door behind the thrones. He waved his hand in front of the door and it opened. He turned and held his hand out,

"Come children; for it is time." Malone and the two sisters walked over too him and followed him into the room.

CHAPTER

5

Inside of the room was a large bed in the middle of the room. He told them to lie down on the bed next to one another. They got up on the bed and lay down next to each other then he walked over to a table. He picked up a challis from a table next to the fireplace and walked over giving each of them a drink. He walked back over to the table and placed the challis back on the table. He turned around and walked back over to them.

He first stood beside Linda, and he placed his hand over her head. She closed her eyes and drifted off to sleep. He slowly moved his hand down to her abdomen and stopped as his hand started to glow. Six ghostly images came out of her and into his hand. He closed his hand and threw them into the fire like he was throwing a base ball. The ghostly images exploded like tinny firecrackers in the fire.

Malone got up on her elbows watching as he removed the demon seeds from Linda,

"My God." The Lord looked at her with a smile on his face as he continued to work on Linda. Massaging her abdomen from a few inches above her,

"Close, very close. But there is only one. He allows me to do his work for him. For he is and always has and always will be the only one." Then he looked back down at Linda and his hand stopped glowing.

By then, Pinkie had also faded off to sleep from the drink she took from the challis. Malone was feeling a little groggy herself and laid back down. Pinkie was fast asleep, and the Lord put his hand over her head. He moved his hand down to her abdomen like he'd done to Linda. The seeds within her had also come out of her and into his hand. He had cast them into the fire just as he had cast the ones from Linda.

Malone laid there as he walked around to the side of her. She watched as he put his hand over her forehead. She gasped and felt her body arch upwards. He closed his eyes and started praying because he felt the evil in her was very strong and didn't want to leave her. He moved his hand and leaned over,

"Child; when you walked into the cult temple did you mumble the words on the wall?" she thought about it and turned to face him.

"Yes; yes I did. But they were only words; I didn't think anything of it." He looked at her with a hurtful look on her face and bowed his head. A tear fell from each of his eyes and rolled down his cheeks. He looked ay her,

"Child; when you spoke those words; you denounced and cursed the father and myself." He turned and walked over to a table under a cross and picked up a book. He walked back over to her and asked her to place her right hand on the book. She put her hand on the book and he closed his eyes and began to pray. He opened his eyes and looked at her,

"Child; close your eyes and say theses words aloud." A loud boom was heard above them. Barstow knocked franticly on the door,

"Lord! Lord! We're being attacked." He told Malone to stay where she was and rest. He left the room and closed the door behind him.

Malone laid there thinking about what he'd said about the temple. She remembered the temple and the blood that covered the walls in the basement. She also remembered that she lost her first partner to a bullet from one of the misguided teenagers in the temple. She also remembers what he said to her as he laid on the floor dieing from the bullet she put in him.

"You'll never escape him; he'll always be with you; you forsook and accepted." Then he stopped breathing. She seen the look on his face as he was laying there dieing from her bullet. He looked as if he was enjoying his death.

Up stairs Michael was standing next to the doorway. He was watching as Balentar and a group of strange looking people throwing large rocks at the church. For some reason they wouldn't come any closer. They seem to be afraid of the church and wouldn't come past the same rock as the small dog. He looked at the dog which was standing next to him. The dog was growling at the people outside.

The Lord and Barstow immerged from the stairwell. They walked over to Michael and stood beside him. The Lord walked onto the stoop at the front door and stood there. He raised his hands out at his side. One of the strangers picked up and threw a large rock at him. The Lord had seen the rock heading for him and put his right hand out at the rock. The rock just seem to stop in midair and crumble into a million pieces.

Balentar smiled and looked at the Lord. He started laughing, and all of those who were with him cowered down and huddled together with fear. The Lord looked at them and asked,

"Why do you wish to harm these people? Go; leave in peace!" Balentar laughed and tried to come closer, but the clearing acted as a shield keeping him out. The Lord stepped down off of the stoop and walked over towards them. He stopped close to the edge of the clearing and looked at each of them. He asked,

"What evil that cometh to your hearts, is not the evil which dwelleth at your birth to this world." The strangers all still cowering understood what he was saying and stood up. Balentar didn't like that he spoke to them and calmed them down. He turned to them in anger he let out a roar, thrusting his hands towards them fire from his hands engulfed them. The screams were agonizing as they reverted back to their human forms.

As they passed away, the Lord held his hands out and waited until their spirits left their bodies. As soon as their spirits exited their charred body, the Lord held out his hands. He welcomed them across the border of the clearing. He was smiling as they crossed over to him. He turned and led them into the church. On the way to the church, they seem to change into human form. As they entered the church, Balentar got so angry he tried his best to get through the border. He was kept out by the power which protects all of them from evil.

Barstow and Michael were standing next to each other as the spirits walked inside. They stopped and kneeled down in front of them. They started weeping and asked for forgiveness. Michael stepped forward and put his hand on the shoulder of the one of the spirits. Michael smiled as he looked up at him,

"It's ok; it wasn't your fault you couldn't control what happened. I forgive you!" The Lord walked over and stood there smiling. Because even though they were being chased by them, Michael still had enough heart to forgive his pursuers. Barstow also felt that it wasn't their fault and walked over beside Michael. He told them,

"I don't understand; you are all soldiers. Your uniform insignia tells me that you're the best of the best. I forgive you and hope that God allows you to rest in peace." Both Barstow and Michael stood side by side as the Lord walked over to them and the spirits stood up and followed him to the door on the far side of the church. He waved his hand in front of it and it opened. A light shined brightly from the room. He looked at them and smiled,

"Walk into the light my children; you have been forgiven and shall join your loved ones." Gabriel walked over to them and smiled as he looked at them and then the Lord. He looked back at them and said,

"Come with me and I shall guide you to the other side, and I shall remain with you for your transition." Gabriel reached out his hand and took one of them by the hand. The soldier who Gabriel took by the hand reached out and took the hand of another as did he until all of them joined hands and walked into the light.

After the last soldier walked into the light, the Lord closed the door. Then he walked over to the stairwell and walked down to finish his work with Malone. Barstow and Michael went over to the stairwell and looked down to see the Lord walk out of their sight. They were hesitant and a little scared about following him because he'd told them to wait where they were.

CHAPTER

6

Michael heard Balentars voice speaking to him. He looked at Barstow who kept looking down in the stairwell. Over and over Balentar called out for Michael. He walked over to the doorway and looked out at him. He didn't look like he did a little while ago, he looked like his Grandfather.

Michael walked outside and towards the edge of the clearing, stopping just out of Balentars reach. He stood there looking at him with disbelief that it was his Grandfather.

"Grandpa? Is that you?"

"Yes Michael it is." In a loving tone. He smiled at Michael.

"Come here and let Grandpa give you a big hug." Michael smiled and backed up a few feet. And stood there looking at Balentar.

Barstow noticed Michael was outside speaking to Balentar. He ran out side and got into the troop carrier. He climbed through the hatch on the top of the carrier and cocked the machinegun. Barstow open fire on

Balentar hitting him repeatedly. Michael watched as Balentar reverted back to his demon form. Balentar fell backwards hitting the ground. As Balentar lay on the ground, Barstow yelled to Michael,

"Run Michael; back into the church. Hurry Michael run, run." Michael turned around and ran into the church. Barstow climbed out of the hatch onto the top of the carrier and jumped off. Running for the safety of the church he all of the sudden stopped when he heard the voice of his mother. He turned around and looked at her then over at Balentar still lying on the ground.

"Jonathan I'm scared. Why were those people trying to hurt you?" Barstow looked at his mother and wept. He walked over to her and dropped to his knees. He wrapped his arms around her waist with his head up against her. Barstow didn't notice that he'd crossed the safety of the clearing.

His mother's voice turned from a concerned mother voice to a hideous gurgling. Barstow slowly looked up to see that the image of his mother was Balentar. His eyes were filled with fear. He loosened his hold and tried to get back across the edge of the clearing. But Balentar grabbed him by his ankle and pulled him back. Barstow started screaming as he struggled to escape but Balentar was too strong.

Michael ran back outside to see his father was fighting for his life. He ran over towards him to try to help him. Barstow yelled,

"No son; don't come any closer." Balentar picked him up by his ankle and carried him away over his shoulder. Barstow reached out his hands,

"I love you son; always remember daddy loves you." Then Balentar disappeared into the woods with Barstow over his shoulder. Michael stood there crying as his father disappeared out of sight.

Michael ran back into the church and down the stairwell. He didn't stop until he'd gotten to the door of the bed chamber where the Lord, Malone and the two sisters were. The door was closed and Michael started beating on it for what seems like hours. But nobody opened the door to see him as he sat on the floor crying over his father's abduction. He sat there on the floor unaware he was being watched by an angel he would later in his life come to meet. The angel too started weeping from his pain.

As the angel kept watch over Michael, inside the bed chamber the Lord stood over Malone as she slept. He placed his hand over her forehead and prayed as she slept. He stopped praying and walked over to a wall where two daggers and a short sword hung on the wall. He took the daggers and sword down and walked back over to her.

Laying the sword and one of the daggers on the bed beside her, he held one of the daggers in his finger tips and prayed. When he finished praying, he placed the dagger on her body between her breast and stomach pointing towards her stomach. Then he picked up the other dagger and did the same placing it across the other forming a cross. He picked up the sword and placed it between her legs, pointing towards her vagina. He placed his hands one over her forehead the other over the cross of daggers. His hands started glowing very brightly and the cross's started vibrating. The sword levitated just a few inches above her body.

As he stood there he closed his eyes and prayed. He slowly moved his hands down her body stopping over her abdomen. The evil seeds fought to stay inside of her, but the powers of Heaven was at work on her. One by one the evil seeds came out of her body screaming and cursing the Lord as he expelled them from her. Each of the evil seeds were impelled by the sword. The last of the seeds spoke. It laughed as it said,

"My father who are not of heaven taketh his trophy that you could not protect. It was not the little one named Michael he was after, it was his father." The sword impelled the last one then flew into the fire. After they had become no more, the sword and daggers placed them selves back on the wall where they belonged. The Lord was pleased that the evil seeds were no longer a threat to the world.

The angel whom had seen Michael appeared in the bed chamber. She told him of the events that took place while he was with Malone and the two sisters. He looked at the angel and told her,

"Nadeema; you are charged with the care of the three women. They must never know what has happened to them. I shall turn back the hands of time and place them in separate lives. Michael will be their key stone in which they shall become close to him." Nadeema bowed her head and said,

"I understand Lord, for the one I hold dear to my heart shall be protected. He shall never know what has happened." She went over to the bed and leaned over kissing each one of them on the forehead. The spot where she kissed them on the forehead glowed for a few seconds then a small cross like mark appeared on the back of their neck.

Nadeema waited as the three of them awoke into a Trans like state. They sat up on the bed as Nadeema watched them. The Lord opened the door to see Michael sitting on the floor just outside. He kneeled down and picked him up. As he stood there holding Michael in his arms, Nadeema motioned the three to follow her. She followed as the Lord walked back up the stairs to the floor above. They walked out the front door into the clearing and the doors to the church closed. The troop carrier disappeared and trees grew quickly in front of the church, hiding it from sight.

Nadeema led the three through the woods and the Lord placed Michael on the ground. He stood there and prayed as he looked down at Michael. The Lord just seemed to disappear seconds before an ambulance pulled up. Nadeema stopped within sight of Michael and a tear trickled down her cheek as they put Michael on the gurney.

"Fear not; for I shall see you again my love." As they put him into the ambulance and drove off she watched as they drove out of sight. She turned to the three and continued through the woods taking them to LA where they would live to serve as care takers for Michael. They would never know the life they once lived elsewhere.

CHAPTER

7

Michael arrived at the sisters of mercy hospital. He was in a coma and had no identification telling who he was. The police were called to the hospital along with social services. They took photos of him along with fingerprints. They waited for someone to come forward to identify him, but nobody came forward.

The whole time he was in the hospital Nadeema was there watching over him. Nobody could see her as she sat there holding Michaels hand. The only reason nobody came forward, no television set except for Malone and the two sisters could see that it was Michael. All of the other television sets revealed the appearance of a child long sense passed away some two hundred years ago.

For some strange reason he seem to be familiar to them. Something about him was like a dream that they shared; a dream that was oh so real. They couldn't figure out why it was so important that they go to Michael. Some of the dreams were so real to them, they seen each other. Some were good dreams; others were nightmares which woke them from their sleep. Their husbands were concerned about them and their jobs were affected severely.

Malone was working as a research assistant in a biological laboratory in the San Francisco area. Her boss had seen a dramatic change in her over the course of just a few weeks. She dressed more provocatively and was making advances towards not only the men in the lab but the women as well. She seemed to be changing into a totally different person.

One afternoon she watched as one of her coworkers went into the ladies room. She waited for two or three minutes then went into ladies room. She locked the door behind her and walked over to the intercom and turned up the volume a little bit. The music that was playing was a continuance loop with no pauses.

Malone took out a vial from her purse and opened it. The lid had a sponge swab in it which was saturated with the chemical in the vial. The chemical was something she'd developed in the lab and kept a secrete from ever one. She'd been waiting for this moment to get her alone for two weeks. Ever sense she found the photos of her husband and her having intercourse with two other women. Her coworker's purse was sitting on the counter and she knew this was her opportunity to do what she had to do.

She thought about her children as she made sure that their father would never cheat on her again. Now it was time that she made sure that her coworker would never be part of an affair again. The anger was so intense; she felt her skin crawling. She reached into her coworker's purse and took out the tube of lipstick. Malone looked over at the stall door while she opened the lipstick and smeared the chemical on it. She closed the tube and placed it back into her purse.

Malone heard the lock on the stall door slide open. She looked in the mirror to see her walk out of the stall. She looked hung over from a night at a bar that ladies go to meet other ladies. Malone knows of her sexual preference; and used it to her advantage. She waited till she was next to her at the sink and turned around and sat down on the counter. She smiled at her and looked her up and down.

She looked at her for a second or two and reached out to stroke her hair. She closed her eyes as Malone stroked her hair grasping Malone's wrist. She asked,

"I noticed you wear a ring; is that a ring of marriage; or of partnership?" Malone smiled then leaned forward and kissed her.

"What do you think?" they chuckled a little. The woman reached into her purse and took out a pad of paper. Writing down her name and number on the paper and folded it in half. She looked at Malone's breasts as she tucked the paper in between them.

"Call me; if you're not busy tonight we can do what ever comes to mind. I have two other women living with me and we share everything together. You're Spanish; aren't you? We love Spanish food; we love to eat it up." She took out her lipstick and put a coat of it on her lips. Malone smiled as she put her poison on her lips.

"Do you share everything; even that lipstick on your luscious lips?" She smiled and licked her lips which made the poison work even faster. Malone scooted back on the counter against the mirror and put her knees up. She didn't have any panties on and pulled her skirt up to interest her. She was so interested she swallowed and took a deep breath,

"By the way; if you're interested; I know this guy who really gets into threesomes; or are ah; are you strictly into women?" Malone smiled at her,

"Why don't you invite your boy over and we'll see if I like his toy and see if you and your boy toy likes this toy." She smiled at Malone and wrote her address on another piece of paper.

"Here's my address; it's pretty easy to find. The whole place is sound proof so the neighbors can't hear anything once I close my door. If you want, we quit in a half of an hour; we can shower at my place and have dinner." Malone puckered her lips,

"That sounds like a beautiful idea Sandy. I'll get my things together and join you there." Sandy was giddy and thought she'd been given a new toy for her pleasure. She unlocked the bathroom door and walked out. Malone's face quickly changed from all smiles to a look that could kill. The way she feeling about the whole situation made her stomach turn.

She's been thinking about how to put her plan into effect; and she didn't know that it would be easy. To have the opportunity fall in her lap so easy was truly what she'd been looking for. She never thought that the chemical compound she'd been working on in secrete would come in handy as a weapon. What she'd developed was at first a cure for the cancer cells in the body. She had everything a woman could ever want in life, A house with the classic white picket fence; three wonderful children and a dog; that was more faithful than her husband.

But that all ended two weeks ago she found out that Sandy and two other women have been having an affaire with her husband. She found pictures of him with her and another women in bed together having intercourse. Malone doesn't show how she truly feels; she's good at hiding her feelings. Even her husband doesn't know that her heart has been shattered.

The fortunate part for Malone; is she doesn't know that she is married to the man she's having the affair with. All she knows is that Malone is a stone cold Spanish fox. Malone has been dosing her husband with large quantities of the compound sense she'd found out about the affair. By now his body is so toxic; if he were dosed with anything other than the compound she developed; he'd be dead.

The thing about the compound; is it works on the sexual organs only. Once she introduced the compound into both her husband and her body two weeks ago; she knows it won't be long before it does its job. No matter how good the corner or any one else is; they'll never find a trace of the compound. The only conclusion they'll be able to come to is they screwed to death.

Malone left work and went to her aunt's car parked in the parking garage. When she got in she sat there crying because of what she'd done. Something about what she'd done with Sandy felt good to her deep down inside. She had momentary outbursts of smiles and laughter. She put her finger across her lips and between her teeth. She kept thinking about how good Sandy looks and her naked body in those pictures.

She knows just from seeing the pictures then meeting her; she'd made a mistake. She went back into her office and sat down at her desk. She unlocked the security drawer and took out a vial she had hidden away. The vial was the antidote for the death serum she laced her lipstick with. She ran out of the office and back to her car. She waited till she seen her come out and get into her car. Then she called her on her cell phone.

"Hey good looking; this is your Spanish desert; I'm right behind you and would like to buy you a drink before we get down to the main course." She saw her look in her mirror and wink.

"Follow me; I know a little out of the way spot the people from work would never see us at." They hung up their phones and Malone followed her out of the garage staying behind her to the parking lot of a motel at the edge of town. Malone pulled into the spot next to her and got out of her car and into Sandy's car.

She locked her door because of the neighborhood. Sandy's windows were dark tinted and hard to see into. Malone took the vial from her pocket opened it and took a drink. Sandy watched as she took a drink,

"What is that; looks good; may I?" Malone handed her the vial and watched as she drank. She smiled and liked her lips,

"That is good; tastes like cherry; oh that's so good does it feel hot in here?" She started unbuttoning her top as Malone watched. She kept her eyes on Malone as she took her top off. She wriggled out of her skirt and reached over taking Malone's hand and guided it to her breast. Malone sat there rubbing her breast then leaned over and kissed her lips with passion. Malone slowly sat back over in her seat and caught her breath,

"Wow; that was; well; it was. Why don't you finish the rest of this and lets see how much more horny you can get." She looked at Malone and smiled,

"Liquid Spanish fly; is that what we are drinking?" Sandy tipped the bottle up and drank the last drop. She seems to be very anxious to get Malone back to her place and told her,

"Hey baby; now that it's dark out; we can go to my place and have sex until one of us drops. So go ahead and get into your car and follow me home." Malone got out of her car and got into her car. They left the parking lot and Malone followed her to her house. As they pulled up to Sandy's house, she saw her husband's car parked in the driveway. Malone watched as Sandy got out of her car and walk up to her house. Sandy motioned for her to come inside and turned around staggering she walked inside. Malone got out of her car and waited for a couple of minutes. She carefully walked up the sidewalk not to let her husband see her.

When she walked inside the house, she heard the sound of a man and woman moaning in ecstasy. Malone walked upstairs and stayed out of sight while she watched as her husband and Sandy were making love. By now the anger had turned to anxiousness to see the compound do its job. She waited and watched as her husband grabbed his chest. She knew that the compound was finally doing what she'd designed it to do.

Malone slipped out of her clothes and walked into the room. Her husband's throat started to close up and the motions he was making; Sandy thought were that of sexual wants. She walked over and stood over top of him so he could see what he threw away. She kneeled down and let him get a good look at her vagina. She kept it in his face as she leaned forward and placed her lips to Sandy's. She kissed Sandy so her husband could see them as he took his last breath looking at the two of them. Malone waited for a few minutes then stood up.

Sandy noticed he wasn't breathing and started screaming. Malone kneeled down and checked his pulse. She started acting like she caused him to have a heart attack; killing him with sex. Sandy kept saying over and over,

"What should I do?" Malone took Sandy into her arms and held her trying to calm her down. She put her finger tips under Sandy's chin and gave her a peck on the forehead. Then she hugged her tightly,

"Now it's just you, me and the other two who were in those pictures." Sandy still in shock over the death of Malone's husband; had no clue what she was saying to her. She took her over and sat her down on the bed. She kneeled down in front of her,

"He was a cheater; he has a wife who took out a rather large insurance policy on him. Do you want to know who his wife is?" She stood up in front of her and took her by the hands,

"Sweat heart, it's me. I am his wife; and his death is our gain. About twenty million dollars worth of gain." She looked at Malone then at him lying on the floor. She smiled and sat there holding Malone's hands. She was stroking Malone's fingers with her finger tips,

"The others in the pictures; were people he knew from San Diego and Las Vegas. Their names are Pinkie and Linda. They were two of the freakiest women I'd ever been with." Malone kneeled down in front of her on one knee and took off her two rings. She slipped her engagement ring onto Sandy's finger. It fit like a glove and made Sandy tingle from Malone's jester.

"I feel so; used by him. I mean; he lied to me the whole time we were together. To lie to me just to get some booty; pisses me off more than any thing." Malone stood up and let her hands go. She turned down the covers on the bed and climbed into the bed between the sheets. She told her to get into the bed with her and go to sleep. Patting the bed, Sandy climbed in with her. Facing Malone she asked,

"What is your first name?" Malone smiled,

"Maria, Maria Malone." Sandy was concerned about what she was going to tell the police. Malone seen this and told her,

"Just keep your mouth shut when they get here and let me do all of the talking. Everything is going to turn out just fine." Malone smiled and reached over and turned out the light.

"How do I know that you won't say I did something to him?" Malone licked her lips and leaned over and started kissing her. She climbed on top of her and started making love to her. They made love until Sandy drifted off to sleep. While Sandy slept, Malone gently slipped the ring off of Sandy's finger and stuck it back on her finger. She took a doily out from under a cosmetic tray she wrapped it around a heavy figurine and hit her husband in the head with it. She dropped it next to him on the floor and went into the hallway bathroom to wash up. Malone put her cloths back on and went down stairs.

The vials the compound she poisoned her husband with was inside of her overnight bag. She put them in the kitchen under the sink next to the drain cleaner. Then she went out to Sandy's car and got the vial that the antidote was in and put it in her pocket. She went around to the passenger side and wiped her finger prints down with a solution that removes all finger print from everything. She looked up at Sandy's bedroom window and took out her cell phone. Malone called the police and reported some noise coming from Sandy's house.

"911; how may I direct your call; Police, Fire or Ambulance?" Franticly Malone told the operator,

"Police; I guess I need the police. I was walking with my lover and saw two people having a fight. I asked my lover if she wanted to help, but she didn't want her husband to find out she was a lesbian. Please hurry; I'm afraid she's going to get hurt." The operator was on the other end of the line trying to calm Malone down,

"Miss; calm down the Police will be there in fifteen minutes. Stay away from the house; do not enter the house under any circumstances." While she was trying to ask Malone for her name, Malone hung up the phone.

CHAPTER

8

Malone got into her car and drifted backwards out of her driveway and down the hill. She started her car and turned around to watch just a few minutes before seven police cars pulled up to Sandy's house. Malone sat there as the police burst into the house. Sandy had woken up minutes before the police arrived and noticed Malone wasn't in bed beside her. She walked over and picked up the figurine and was looking at the gash on his head. The antidote she'd given Sandy had an after effect that was like a hallucinogenic.

She was stooped over him when the police burst into her bed room. She was stunned by the sudden entrance the police made. She fell backwards next to the bed and her hand landed on top of a gun that had slid under the edge of the bed. She picked up the gun to give it to the police, but someone yelled,

"Gun!" The police open fire and shot her several times. Three of the shots hit her in the chest and one in the head. She was killed instantly by the shot to the head. The police holstered their weapons and stood there for a minute. One of the officers checked her for a pulse but pronounced her dead. The officer looked over at Malone's husband lying on the floor. He noticed that he was still erect, he started laughing. As he looked closer at his face he noticed that it was Detective Sergeant Malone.

"Oh shit; we need to call the Captain, he's a cop." The officers cleared out of the bedroom and went back down stairs. One of the officers stayed just outside of the bedroom to guard the crime scene. The others went outside and called for more help. The neighbors already started gathering outside after hearing the gun shots.

Malone was keeping her distance to keep from being seen by the police. She was glad she'd borrowed her aunt's car for the month while she was in Brazil visiting her mother. She watched as more police arrived at Sandy's house and went inside. She started the engine and headed for home as more emergency vehicles were arriving on the scene.

Malone parked two blocks away from he house incase someone seen her aunt's car at Sandy's house. She carefully made her way around to the back of her house. Her children went with her aunt to visit their Grandmother in Brazil. She opened the sliding glass door and crept inside. She picked up the towel she'd left spread out on the floor and wrapped her sex toys in it.

She went upstairs and put them inside of her hope chest. She sat down on the foot of the bed and took out the picture album. She opened it and started looking at the pictures of her children. There were a lot of pictures of all three of her children together and of each of them at birth held by her husband. The phone rang three times before she answered it. The number on the caller ID was from the Chief of Detectives. He called to inform her that her husband died in the line of duty. She was already crying from looking at the pictures which made it easy for her to fake her concern for her husband.

"Hello; Mrs. Malone this is Chief Detective Stone. I'm sorry to have to inform you that your husband has been killed in the line of duty. If there is anything I can do for you; please don't hesitate to ask at any time." She asked him how he had died but he avoided her question. But Malone already knew and played dumb as far as the cause of his death. Malone threw in a few gasps to make it sound good. She thanked him for his concern and hung up the phone. She closed the picture album and put it away.

She walked into the bathroom and turned on the shower. Testing the water to see if it was at the right temperature, she climbed in. As she soaped up she stood there, sick over what she had done with her. It didn't bother her that she set her up to take the fall for her husband's murder. But what bothered her the most; is the life she led before she'd gotten married came out again. She was so disgusted with herself. She tried to but couldn't get rid of the urges she was feeling when she was with her. Even now as she stood there thinking of past lovers. One in particular she fondly remembers; was her college room mate.

She herd that she had a child and right now he'd be around six or seven years old. Sitting down in the shower; her back was against the tub top and the water was dancing off of her breasts. She was crying as she sat there thinking of Babbs. Her head leaned back against the shower wall and she looked out and she tried to get her off of her mind.

The phone rang "Ring, Ring, Ring!" as the phone rang; she got up and stepped out of the shower. She picked up the phone and looked at the caller ID. The number was the Sisters of Mercy Hospital. She was dripping water from the shower she was taking; she walked back into the bathroom and stepped back into the tub. She reached up and adjusted the shower head down. Sitting back down; she answered the phone.

"Hello; yes this is Maria Santiago; yes I do know a Babbs Conswella." When the hospital told her what had happened; she rinsed off and got dressed. She raced out of the house and went down the block to her aunt's car. She got in and drove to the hospital. On the way to the hospital, she kept thinking who it was Babbs said she'd gotten married to.

"I know his name started with a T; Tolman; Tillan; Talon. Yeah Talon was his name; Ronnie Talon." She kept thinking about how she'd told her that he always spoke about Spanish women always turned him on. A smile came to her face as she drove towards the Hospital. With her being Spanish; she knew exactly what she meant. There's a saying in Brazil,

"Once a Spanish woman lets you into her bed; you stay there until you're dead." She pulled into the parking garage and gat out of the car. A teenager; around eighteen years old who was walking by her stopped dead in his tracks.

She kept walking; even though he kept saying some rude remarks to her. She took for granted his age had a lot to do with his lack of respect for her or any other women. When she got into the elevator she kind of smiled because of some of the things he'd said. They were some of the things she loves to hear. She thought to herself that if he's still here when she comes back to her car; he's going to get very lucky.

Before the elevator door closed she put her arm in the way which stopped the door from closing. She pointed the remote at the car and pushed the button. The car alarm tweaked and the lights flashed. She looked at him and bit down on her lower lip,

"Hey you; yeah you; get in the car and wait here for me. If your still here when I get back; you'll never find anyone who can do what I'll do with you." The teenager almost broke his neck to get in the car as fast as he could. She smiled and stepped back to let the elevator door close.

As the elevator climbed upwards; she thought about Babbs son. She was thinking the worse about his condition. What had happened to him; and what he was going to look like when she sees him for the first time? The elevator stopped and the door opened. She left the elevator and went over to the nurse's station.

"Excuse me nurse; can you help me please?" when the nurse looked up Maria was standing there with her hands on the counter. She stood up and smiled at her; she couldn't take her eyes off of her.

"You look very familiar too me for some reason. I know you from somewhere; I know I do; but where?" Maria looked at her and started thinking she also looked familiar. Then it came to her; she was one of the girls who were at her all night women's party a few years ago when her husband went to Vegas. She didn't say that's where she knew her from; she didn't want to strike up a conversation about the party. She was here for Michael; not for her own personal affairs.

She couldn't help but to keep thinking about the nurse's question. Her thoughts turned to feelings of worry and she felt the walls closing in on her. She looked around and seen everyone staring at her. She felt a chill come over her and her palms started to sweat. She wiped her palms on her skirt and crossed her arms as she stood there nervous from the stares.

The nurse walked out from behind the nurse's station and tapped her on the shoulder. She jumped out of her skin and squealed from the surprise of her touching her. She asked kept her hand on Malone's shoulder and put her other hand on her forearm. Malone had a tear in her eye from the sudden shock and laughed as she put her hand to her mouth.

"Are you ok? I didn't mean to scare you." Malone put her hand on her arm and bowed her head. She looked at the nurse and asked her,

"Are you here for someone in particular?" Malone leaned her head back and opened her eyes. Lowering her head she looked at her and licked her lips. She shuffled around and reached out taking her hands. While holding her hands she told her,

"You're right; you do know me; but I need to ask you to do me a favor." She smiled and shuffled side to side feeling giddy as a school girl. She looked at her and said to her,

"I thought that I was right. The minute I saw you, I thought that I felt something." Malone smiled and pulled her closer to her. She leaned against the counter letting one of her hands go and picked up the file on the count. The name on it was John Doe with a line through it. Michael Talon was hand written beside it.

Malone smiled at her,

"This young man is my friend's son." She rubbed the palm of her hand with her thumb. The nurse started feeling sexual feelings for her and asked,

"Any thing you need me to do; the pleasure will be mine." Malone led her to an examination room. When they went in she closed the door behind them. The nurse sat on the examination table and started to take off her clothes. Malone tuned around and saw her,

"What do you think you're doing?" She looked at her seductively with her top off. Her breasts were the largest she'd ever seen before. She was at a loss for words being stunned by the sight of her breasts. She put her knuckle in her mouth and bit down. The nurse put her hands under her breasts and pushed up on them.

"Do you like these? I had them enlarged six months after the party. The one when you told me my body would be perfect if I get them enlarged, so I did." Malone walked over to her and pulled her top closed. She found it hard to control her hormones and her feelings seeing her sitting there like she was. The nurse was stunned that Malone covered her up.

"What I want from you is a favor; there's a young man about your age;" she walked around her and stood behind her. She put her hands on her shoulders and leaned over and whispered into her ear,

"He's in my car down in the garage; do what he wants and then some." She turned her head to look at Malone. She smiled and bit softly on her lower lip. Malone smiled back at her as the nurse slid off of the table. The nurse turned around and got a strange look on her face. She puckered her lips and tilted her head as she looked at Malone,

"Ok; I'll screw him like a pro; but when I'm done and if I can still walk; you sweetie; are mine." Malone felt a little intimidated by her demand and for the first time in her life; she felt like she lost control of the situation. The nurse got a mad look on her face and Malone shook her head yes. Malone closed her eyes in a blinking motion and put her palms together placing them to her mouth. The nurse reached down as she disgustedly looked at Malone and turned the doorknob. Opening the door she told her,

"I'll do what you want; but remember the deal as you visit with Michael; I'll be back for payment." Malone shook her head yes and the nurse walked out. Malone sighed a sigh of relief as the nurse walked out of the room. Malone walked over to the door and cracked it open watching her walk past the nurse's station and into the elevator. As the elevator door closed Malone left the examination room. She walked slowly over to the nurse's station and asked the nurse who sat behind the desk,

"Talon; Michael Talon; what room is he in?" She looked up at her and with a snooty attitude she put her fingertip on the bridge of her glasses and slid them down. She stood up and smacked her lips as she said,

"And just who are you to this young man; and why did you wait this long to visit him?" Malone looked at her and put her tong against the inside of mouth wall and pushed against it. She snickered,

"What the hell are you; a fucking detective; or a bitch with a stick stuck where the sun never gets a chance to show it's face?" She got nervous as Malone spoke to her like that. She sat back down and fidgeted nervously with some papers trying not to show her fear for Malone. She looked on her clipboard and seen Michael's name and room number. But beside it was a notation in red; "restricted; no visitors." She was shaking when she looked up at Malone and started to speak. Malone grabbed the clipboard from her hand,

"Restricted; no visitors; what the hell does that mean?" Malone huffed as she slammed the clipboard down. A doctor was walking towards her so she grabbed him and shoved the clipboard at him. She stood there as he looked at her then at the clipboard,

"And just what am I looking for miss?" She looked at him and yanked the board from his hand. She pointed to Michael's name,

"Restricted; and no visitors; you mean to tell me I can't see my God son?" He leaned towards her to see the notations. He scrunched his chin and a frown on his lips,

"I'm sorry; but that's what the notations mean. He can't under any circumstances have any visitors." Malone got so steamed; she got red in the face.

Nadeema; was appearing to everyone as a nurse. This gave her the freedom to move among everyone in the hospital. When Michael came into the hospital; she was with him the whole time. At will she was able to change her appearance to keep people from seeing her there all the time. She walked over to the doctor and put her hand on his forearm. He felt something calming feeling as if he had somewhere that he had to be. He turned and walked away from her; that only agitated Malone even more. She moved towards Malone and reached out touching her on the forearm.

Malone calmed down and looked at Nadeema in a loving fashion. She started weeping and bowed her head closing her eyes. Nadeema walked her over to the waiting room where she could be by herself. She sat Malone down in a seat in the corner of the room and sat down next to her. Malone hesitated lifting her head to look at Nadeema. When she finally lifted her head; she had red eyes from crying so much. She knew that she was more than a nurse; she knew that she could confide in her.

Malone couldn't find the words to start telling her what she had to say. But Nadeema had already known everything that happened to her sense she had been switched into her life here. Nadeema put her hand on Malone's shoulder,

"I know and understand. You don't have to say anything." Malone put her head on Nadeema's shoulder and wept. Nadeema put her hand on Malone's head,

"It's going to be alright child; it's up to you to change you life and your future. Remember; God loves you; and did what he did for you." Malone slowly sat up and looked at Nadeema; she was sniffling from crying so much. Nadeema smiled and tilted her head as she started telling her about why she was there with Michael.

As she sat there with her hours had passed and she told her some things that seemed so unbelievable to her. Nadeema explained to her about Balentar and everything else surrounding the events, which led her to here. She couldn't believe that she had only lived her present life for such a short time. She seemed to be intrigued by what Nadeema had told her and believed every word uttered from her lips.

While they sat there, a little old lady walked up to them. Nadeema looked up and her and smiled. Malone watched as Nadeema stood up and offered her seat to the woman. Nadeema seem to have a glow to her, as the woman sat there with Malone. She was the classic old lady, wearing a sweater and holding a handbag on her lap.

She put her hand on Malone's knee and patted her like a grandmother would her granddaughter. She started to say something but stopped and looked up at Nadeema,

"Did you tell her why I'm here sweetie?" Nadeema put her hand on the woman's shoulder and nodded. She turned back to Malone and got a serious look on her face,

"What Nadeema has told you, is true sweetie. You were placed into this life by God himself." Malone interrupted her in the middle of what she was telling her. Malone stood up and walked away from her shaking her head. She folded her arms as she looked out of the window. The woman looked at Nadeema,

"I don't believe she fully understands or believes we're telling her. Maybe a miracle of sorts is in order." Nadeema shook her head and turned towards Malone. Slowly she walked over to Malone and stood next to her at the window. She looked out of the window and softly told Malone,

"If I could prove to you what has been said is true, would you then believe?" Malone looked at her and shook nodded her head. Nadeema looked up to the sky and a gentle smile came to her face. She bowed her head and started praying for the night sky to turn to daylight. As she prayed for daylight, the sky started growing lighter. Malone looked at her watch,

"That's impossible, it's ten o'clock at night. How could; oh my God; it's true isn't it?" Nadeema nodded her head and walked back over to the woman. She stood beside the woman and looked at Malone. As Malone turned around, she saw the two of them looking at her. They were smiling and a beautiful light blue glow surrounded them.

Malone put her hands to her mouth and stood there crying. She knew that what they told her was the truth. She dropped to her knees and asked them to forgive her for her ignorance. The woman looked at Nadeema, who looked at Malone,

"Child; it is not your fault that you did not believe us, you just needed a little push in the right direction." Nadeema walked over and helped her to her feet. The two of them walked back over and Malone sat down next to the woman. The old lady smiled and put her arm around Malone. Malone hung her head down feeling like a heathen. She asked in a soft voice,

"How could you ever forgive me for not believing you? I would like to know; who am I?" Malone bowed her head as she wept and kept asking for forgiveness. As they sat there, the old woman put her hand under Malone's chin and lifted her head up to let Malone see her smile.

"Dear child; when I passed on to live for eternity in heaven; my grandson did not believe that I had passed away." The old lady opened her purse and reached inside. She took out a picture of Malone holding Michael as an infant. The old lady was standing behind them with her hands on Malone's shoulders. Malone looked closely at the picture and asked her,

"Why am I in this picture; and who is this child I'm holding? And you're; you're in it to." The old lady and

Nadeema looked at each other and Nadeema sat down on the other side of Malone. The old woman began to explain to Malone how she came to be in the picture. As they sat there a nurse came into the room and saw Malone talking to her self. She backed back out of the room before Malone could see her. The nurse stood just out of sight and listened to what she was saying. Malone was unaware that she had a spectator listening, but Nadeema had seen the nurse and excused her self. She got up and walked past the nurse and stood behind her.

As Malone and the old woman talked, Nadeema took human form and tapped the nurse on the shoulder. The nurse was startled and jumped out of her skin. She let out a squeal and put her hand over her mouth. She chuckled and said,

"You scared me; I ah; I just." She cleared her throat and looked down at the floor. Nadeema smiled,

"May I help you with something; other than listening in on something private? Don't you have duties and rounds to attend to?" The nurse shook her head and looked down as she walked away. Nadeema watched as she walked away bowing her head and praying that she'd forget what she seen. She paused and leaned against the nurse's station as she lost her balance. Nadeema walked over to her and took her by the arm,

"Are you alright nurse? Do you need a doctor?" She looked at Nadeema,

"No; no I'll be alright. I just lost my balance; I'm ok now." Nadeema walked her over to a chair and sat her down. Nadeema smiled and walked away from her as she sat there with her head hung down. As Nadeema walked away, she vanished from sight. The nurse started getting her senses back and looked but Nadeema was nowhere in sight. As the nurse sat there, she felt a chill come over her. The chill she felt was that of Nadeema passing by her on the way back to the waiting room. She rubbed her arms and looked around as Nadeema passed by her. She stood up and put her finger tips on her forehead,

"What was I;I ah?" She looked at her clipboard and answered her own question she was asking herself. Nadeema had a smile on her face, knowing that her prayer had been answered. Nadeema watched her as she'd walked down to the end of the hallway and stopped outside of one of the rooms. She looked back towards Nadeema and hesitated for a few seconds. She opened the door and walked into the room shaking her head because she had a strange feeling that she couldn't explain.

Nadeema walked back into the waiting room as the old woman and Malone was finishing up their conversation. Nadeema stood just inside of the doorway and watched as the old lady and Malone stood up and hugged. The old woman walked over to Nadeema and hugged her. When she finished hugging Nadeema, she held her handbag with both hands and slowly walked out of the room. Stopping in the doorway to turn and look at Malone one last time before walking away.

Nadeema turned to Malone as Malone walked up to her with teary eyes. She put her arms around Nadeema and squeezed her.

"Thank you. Thank you for everything. I understand and want my life back; the one I belong in." Nadeema closed her eyes and bowed her head beginning to pray, but she was interrupted by a commotion outside of the waiting room. Malone looked out into the hallway and saw Pinkie standing near the nurse's station. She was giving the duty nurse a real ruff way to go. Nadeema walked out into the hall and looked at Pinkie, she was invisible to all in the hall. Nadeema walked over to Pinkie and stood beside her. Pinkie felt Nadeema standing there but couldn't see her. Nadeema put her hand on Pinkie's back and closed her eye's. She began to pray for Pinkie to calm her spirit and alter her tone.

The duty nurse got up while Pinkie wasn't paying attention and quickly walked down the hallway. She went into the security office and came back out with two security officers. The nurse and security officers approached Pinkie and stood next to her. One of the security officers asked,

"Excuse me miss; your manner of speech and treatment towards this nurse is inexcusable and can not be tolerated in this or any other hospital. I'm only going to ask you one time to lower your voice and speak to this nurse calmly." Pinkie shook her head yes and felt flushed from being spoken to like a child by the security officer. Nadeema was still standing beside of Pinkie; she pushed on her back and told her to do as they asked her to do. Pinkie put her hands on the nurse's station and hung her head down. Nadeema took her hand off of Pinkie's back and clasped her hands in front of her. Pinkie started to collapse but the two security officers grabbed a hold of her before she fell. They helped her into the waiting room and sat her down on a seat near the doorway.

CHAPTER

9

Malone was standing near the door when they brought he into the room. She looked at Pinkie and thought to herself,

"Something about her looks so familiar; what is it about this woman?" Nadeema walked in and stood beside Malone. No one except Malone could see her standing there. She kept her eyes pined to Pinkie as she leaned towards Malone,

"I would be willing to bet; that is if I was a betting woman; you think that you know her from somewhere, don't you?" Nadeema smiled and Malone looked at Nadeema then back at Pinkie. Nadeema chuckled,

"The woman which you are wondering if you know her; is a very important person in your life. You will probably not be too happy with her if you find out what she had done in your other life. But; if it's the other life you wish to live; then everything shall be as it was." Nadeema put her palm on Malone's forehead and the other on her lower back. Malone felt Nadeema's palms getting hot and began to vibrate with a kind of numbing effect.

Malone felt dizzy and sat down on the seat behind her. Nadeema slowly backed out of the waiting room into the hallway. She stood there for a few seconds and turned to walk away. Nadeema walked down the hall and entered Michael's room. She walked over to Michael and leaned over kissing him on the side of his face. She whispered in his ear,

"My love; we one day will be reunited; when the time is right; all things will be known. Until then; be patient." Then she stood up and looked at him. Nadeema stepped back as the door opened and a nurse entered pushing a cart in front of her. She stopped and walked away from the cart and over to Michael. The nurse took Michael's vitals and reached over him to adjust his oxygen intake. Michael opened his eyes as she was leaning over him and made a sound. It startled her and she had gotten so excited she slipped but caught herself before she fell on him. She ran out of the room saying over and over,

"Oh my God, oh my God." A couple of minutes later a doctor and several nurses came running into Michael's room. They didn't see his eyes open but seen tears in the corner of his eyes. They kept saying his name to see if he would respond to them. He never moved or said a word in response to their pleas for him to say something to them. Nadeema waited as they gave up trying to get a response from him. The doctor looked at the nurses and had gotten so upset at the nurse that had taken Michael's vitals; he gave her the coldest stair she'd ever gotten before. He told her,

"Next time you alert the staff of a patient coming out of a coma; even if that patient so much as twitches a nose hair; alert the janitor." Then he left slamming the door behind him. One of the nurses gave her the same stair as she left the room. The last nurse to leave the room smiled as she put her hand on the nurse's wrist,

"Don't worry about it Hun; I believe you. The first time I had a coma patient on my watch; said hello then went back to sleep. That was ten years ago; and he's still in a coma two doors up the hall on the right." The vitals nurse had a tear in the corner of her eyes. She felt like no one believed her even the nurse who was talking to her. She felt like she was just being nice to her because of the way the doctor spoke to her. The nurse was older and once felt the way the vitals nurse feels. She looked at her watch,

"Listen sweetie; our shift ends in twenty five minutes. Why don't we go down to the cafeteria and have us a cup of coffee; and maybe we can get you through this little bump in the road." The vitals nurse shook her head yes and looked at the older nurse smiling trying to hold back the tears. The older nurse left the room closing the door behind her. The vitals nurse walked over to Michael. She stood there looking at him for a minute thinking that something about him looked familiar. She turned and took hold of her cart pushing it over to the door. She turned and looked once more at Michael before she left the room.

Nadeema had a tear in the corner of her eye from the way the vitals nurse was spoken to. She went over to the door and put her hand on the doorknob and turned it pulling the door open. She peeked out into the hall to see the vitals nurse slowly pushing the cart back to the storage room. Nadeema took human form and walked out into the hallway. Nadeema walked back down the hallway to the waiting room where Malone was sleeping soundly.

When Nadeema saw Malone sleeping, she sat down beside her and looked over at Pinkie. Pinkie looked at Nadeema,

"Do I know you from somewhere? Something tells me I do; but I can't quite place you." Nadeema smiled at her and shrugged her shoulders. Pinkie got up and walked over to Nadeema, she sat down beside Nadeema.

Pinkie leaned forwards looking at Malone,

"Yes; yes I do know you and her too. What's her name?" Nadeema looked at her, "If I told you a story; would you keep an open mind; or would you be negative and disbelieve anything that I tell you?" Pinkie squinted her eyes then closed them bowing her head,

"What you are going to tell me; will it explain why the feelings of not belonging here; would it let me know why I keep having these dreams of somewhere I've never been before." As Nadeema sat there with her, she began to explain why she felt that she didn't belong. As she started to tell her of her real life she was taken from, she heard Linda at the nurse's station.

Nadeema excused herself and stood up. She walked out into the hallway to see that Linda was standing there inquiring about Michael. Nadeema walked over to Linda,

"Hello; may I be of assistance?" Linda turned to Nadeema and as she looked at Nadeema,

"Do; do I know you? I'm sorry but something about you seems so familiar." Nadeema smiled then chuckled a little, "I get that a lot here lately; may I help you with your inquiry of mister Talon?" Linda kept looking at Nadeema with that feeling she couldn't shake. Nadeema put her hand on Linda's shoulder,

"Please come with me and I'll explain his condition to you." Linda walked with Nadeema into the waiting room. Pinkie was still sitting two seats from Malone who was still sitting there sound asleep. Nadeema pulled a chair over next to Pinkie and asked Linda to have a seat while she explains every thing to them. Linda sat in the chair Nadeema put beside Pinkie. She closed the door and turned the sign too private. She reached over and woke Malone with a gentle shake. Malone opened her eyes and took a deep breath,

"How long was I asleep?" Still a little groggy she looked around to see Pinkie and Linda sitting in the room with the door closed. Malone looked at Nadeema then at Pinkie and Linda,

"I can't remember where or how; but I know them both." Nadeema cupped her hands down in front of her. Nadeema sat down on the table in front of them and asked them,

"Keep an open mind about what I'm going to tell you. Malone already knows some of what I have to tell you." Nadeema paused for a second; "Michael is the key to why you all are here; all of you have an interment relationship with Michael. The kind of relationship that is of a heavenly nature." Nadeema glanced at each of them then stood back up and paced the floor. Nadeema stopped and turned towards them; she sighed and took a deep breath.

She started telling them about Balentar and the life that they lived their true life. She told them of the plan that God had for each of them and how they would be in danger if they returned to their previous lives. As she continued, time just seemed to go by quickly and the sun was rising before they knew it. They were all so engrossed with what she had told them they never realized that the night had slipped away.

The door opened and the nurse that Malone sent to her car walked into the room. Her hair was a mess and she had a glow about her. She looked at Malone and smiled at her. Nadeema knew by the way that the nurse looked at Malone the young man would not soon forget what Malone indirectly had done for him. Nadeema smiled and asked the nurse,

"Do you believe in miracles? The power of God and what he's capable of?" the nurse looked at Nadeema with a weird stair. Nadeema smiled and walked over too her uttering the words that made her feel a warming feeling inside. She felt woozy and her head started throbbing with a massive headache came over her. Nadeema kept speaking as the nurse dropped to her knees holding her temples with the palms of her hands. When Nadeema finished speaking she kneeled down and helped the nurse to her feet.

Nadeema asked, "are you alright? You fainted and bumped your head." As the nurse stood unsteady on her feet, Nadeema stood beside her holding her by the arm. The nurse slowly got herself together and looked at Malone, Pinkie and Linda,

"Are you here for Michael Talon? The doctor tells me that he's fine except for being in a coma." Malone asked her to have a seat until she was able to keep from falling. She sat down next to Malone. All four of them kept their eye on her. The nurse felt as if she was a pork chop in a dog pin full of pit bulls. Malone asked her,

"Do you remember anything for the past few hours?" she was trying to remember but couldn't account for her whereabouts or what she'd done for the past few hours. Then as if a switch had been flipped on she said,

"Oh my God, my new boyfriend; I left him down in my car." She chuckled, "tied up like he likes it." She smiled and got up almost falling Malone and Nadeema grabbed her to keep her from falling. She felt her balance come back,

"Wow; that felt as good as sex; ah, ah, gotta go." She started to walk out of the waiting room then stopped and turned to face them,

"Before I go; Michael is just down the hall, please visit him; it may help him come out of his coma." Then she turned and walked out. Nadeema waited for her to leave and told them,

"Come with me; Michael awaits and we must join him where he sleeps." Nadeema led them from the waiting room and down the hall too Michael's room.

Michael was lying there so innocently, he was having a dream about everything that had taken place over the last few weeks. Nadeema walked over and stood beside Michael stroking his hair. Malone, Pinkie and Linda all knew that there was a reason they were there, but until they had seen Michael lying there they really didn't know.

Michael opened his eyes and sat up. He seemed to be in a trance like state and stared off into space. He spoke in an adult voice,

"You have all come here today for answers to your questions. The one question you must ask your selves deep down within your soul; are you willing to accept the consequences of what you seek?" They all wished to return to their real lives and looked at each other and back to Michael. Their decision to return to their lives as they were before now had been made. They stood there as Nadeema walked over behind them and slid a chair over to each of them pressing the chairs against the crease in their legs. She asked them to sit down and close their eyes. Slowly Malone, Pinkie and Linda sat down in the chairs. They closed their eyes and leaned their heads back.

The door into the room started to glow and Michael got up out of his bed. He slowly walked over to and stood in front of each of them, starting with Linda then Pinkie then Malone. One by one he placed his palm on their forehead. As he finished he walked back over to the bed and climbed back under the sheets and lay back down on his pillow. He closed his eyes and went back to sleep.

Nadeema stood beside him and waited as Malone, Pinkie and Linda sat sleeping. Outside the sky turned from day to night several times over. When Malone awoke before Pinkie and Linda, she panicked from not knowing where she was. She stood at the foot of the bed and looked at Michael. He seemed to be older than she remembered, much older. He looked to be around eighteen or nineteen years old. Nadeema was still standing beside of him in a sleep trance. Pinkie and Linda woke up and stood up to see Malone looking at Michael. Nadeema awoke and saw them looking at Michael, who had grown to be a man, while they were sleeping.

Nadeema opened her eyes and walked over to the window. She stood there gazing at the scenery outside of the hospital. Pinkie stood up and walked over to the window to stand next to Nadeema. Pinkie looked at Nadeema and asked,

"Who's over there laying on the bed?" Nadeema smiled and took a breath,

"That is Michael; he's waiting for the time to be right and he'll join us." Linda stood up and walked over to Nadeema. She asked Nadeema,

"Why are we all here? The last thing I remember is the church and that hideous Balentar." Nadeema closed her eyes and bowed her head. She began to weep and turned away from the window. Nadeema walked over to Michael and took his hand. Malone stood up and moved over next to Michael. She looked closely at him; something looked very familiar about him. Malone looked over at Nadeema,

"He looks a lot like me when I was younger; doesn't he? I feel as if there is something more." Nadeema smiled at her and reached over taking her by the hand,

"The reason you feel the way you do; is Michael is your natural son. Everything will come back to you; just give it time and you'll begin to remember." Malone looked down at Michael then back at Nadeema. She put her hand on Michael's forehead and brushed his hair.

CHAPTER

10

Michael opened his eyes and looked up at Malone and Nadeema. He tried to speak but his vocal cords were seized up from being in a coma for so many years. Pinkie and Linda herd Michael making sounds as he tried to speak. They walked over too Michael's bedside and were esthetic that he was awake.

Michael motioned for something to write with. He was upset that he couldn't speak and they could tell by the way her pouted. Malone reached over and opened the drawer under the lap tray and found a pen and pad of paper. Malone handed Michael the pen and paper and looked at him as he began to write.

He was frustrated as he tried to write what he wanted to say. Every time he started to write something on the paper he messed up and scratched through it. Malone told him,

"Michael; slow down and take your time and you won't mess up." He looked at her and smiled. He listened to Malone and took his time, thinking about what he wanted to say. He started writing some words on the

114

paper looking up he handed her the paper to show her what he'd written. She looked at the paper and read it. She handed the paper to Nadeema who read it. She looked at Michael,

"Michael; Barstow was taken by Balentar at the church and he hasn't been seen sense." Michael looked over at the door and smiled. He tried to speak, from the movement of his lips he was saying grandma. He held his hands out as tears fell from his eyes. As he lowered his arms he tilted his head like someone was sitting there with their hand on his face.

Nadeema smiled as Michael's grandmother sat on the bed with her hands on his face. She looked at Nadeema and smiled then back at Michael,

"It's time for all things to be put into place and a place for all things to be put." As she finished speaking she stood up and slowly materialized in front of Malone and the two sisters. They were a little frightened at first. It scared Linda so bad she urinated on her self. And her sister fell back over the chair behind her, hitting her head on the wall. Malone put her hands over her mouth and started to weep. As she stood there shaking she walked over and put her arms around her mother.

"Why didn't you go to Heaven mommy?" As she hugged Malone she had also began to weep. She stood there enjoying the moment. She felt the pain Malone had felt for such a long time with her death and when she gave Michael to her sister. She patted Malone on her back and told her,

"Please darling, please don't be sad. The pain in your heart will vanish and you will know in time what must be shall be finally understood by you." Malone didn't understand what she was telling her and felt the sorrow in her heart ease from seeing her mother again.

Malone had a tear of joy trickle down her cheek as her mother put her hand on Malone's right cheek. Malone closed her eyes and grasped her mothers hand as she caressed Malone's check. She sighed and smiled at Malone,

"Sweetheart, always remember I'll be with you and watching over you and Michael. And the answer to your question, Heaven is quite beautiful and waits for every one who believes in it and asks to save them from the furnace of Hell." Malone's mother stepped back a few feet and looked over to her right. She put her hand up to her mouth and scrunched her head into her shoulders with joy.

She looked back at Malone and smiled as she turned to her right and slowly moved towards the window. With every step she took, she seemed to grow denser in solid form. After a few moments and steps she just faded out of sight. They heard her speaking as her voice seemed to also fade,

"Remember, trust only the truth in what you know and the ones whom surround you with love from the heart. Follow your heart and not your mind and all things will become clear in time." Her voice ceased. Nadeema was standing next to Michael as he started writing on the paper. As he wrote he started to utter some words. Slowly his words started becoming clearer to the ear. He looked over at Malone,

"Momma, I know what it is I'm suppose to do. But there's something you and Pinkie and Linda need to also do." They cast their attention towards Michael as he spoke.

"Go home and gather as many believers as you can find. Bring them to the old church and wait there." Malone smiled at Michael and leaned over kissing him on his forehead. Then she turned to Pinkie and Linda and walked over and stood between the two of them. Putting each of her arms over their shoulder,

"Come ladies we have a lot to do and not much time to do it in." Malone looked over her left shoulder and smiled at Michael as she and the two sisters walked out of the room. Michael had a tear come to the corner of his eye's as he thought about what was about to take place. Nadeema put her arms around him to consul him.

She walked over to the window and looked out. As she looked around something caught her attention out of the corner of her eye. Balentar was standing across from the hospital smiling as he looked at her with such an evil stair. Nadeema saw Malone and the two sisters come out of the hospital entrance. But she wasn't the only one, Balentar had also seen them. He looked up at her as she watched helplessly to save them from certain death.

Malone looked over to where Balentar was standing. Something looked familiar about him, as she looked at him it came to her who he is. At abut that time Balentar raised his hand and a ball of fire formed in his hand.

Malone pushed Pinkie and Linda to the ground and jumped on top of them to protect them. He threw it at them missing them and hitting a parked car near them.

Malone felt her pistol on her side. She drew it from her holster aimed and opened fire on Balentar. She hit him four times in the chest and once in the forehead. Balentar fell backwards hitting the ground. As he laid on the ground motionless, she started to walk towards him but stopped when she saw Nadeema banging on the window and motioning to her not to go near him. About that time Balentar sat up and slowly got up on his feet.

Balentar opened his eyes as his head raised. The bullet hole in his forehead seemed to close up. He looked right at Malone and told her,

"I really wish you wouldn't have done that, I was really starting to like you and you just had to go and blow it when you shot me!" Malone didn't know what to do. She looked at Pinkie and Linda and tilted her head with a smile on her face,

"Watch over Michael for me will you!" At that time a small fire ball hit her in the chest and she fell to the ground, her body laid lifeless in front of Pinkie and Linda. They screamed out in sorrow over Malone's death. Balentar laughed and looked up at Nadeema holding up one of his fingers on his left hand then four on his right hand saying,

"One down, and four to go." Then he just vanished from sight.

CHAPTER

11

Pinkie and Linda rushed over to Malone's lifeless body. The street looked like a war zone with Malone the only casualty. Nadeema turned to Michael with tears in her eyes. She couldn't bring herself to tell Michael that his mother had been murdered by the same demon who took his father so many years ago.

Michael stood up next to the bed unsteady on his feet he swayed back and fourth. Reaching out the bed kept him from falling as he made his way towards Nadeema. She stopped him at the end of the bed,

"You don't want to, Michael please sit down." Michael sat back down on the bed and looked at Nadeema. He was weak and tried to get back up on his feet but couldn't. He felt a knot in the pit of his stomach, the kind of knot that you feel when something scares you. Nadeema helped him back into bed and pulled the covers back over him. Michael reached out and grasped the wrist of Nadeema and looked at her with tears in his eyes,

"When she died; did she suffer?" Nadeema reached over and brushed his hair with her finger tips. A tear trickled from her eye and down her cheek,

"She died with honor and with dignity saving the lives of Pinkie and Linda. Balentar tracked the four of you here and he was waiting for them when they left." Michael started praying and asked for GOD to welcome and watch over his mother in heaven.

In the corner of the room he saw Malone and his grandmother. They smiled at him then a man appeared behind them. The man stepped in front of them and looked at Nadeema then at Michael. He was dressed in a white robe reaching out he touched Michael on the side of his face.

"Michael my faithful servant; I heard the prayer for your mother and she shall be welcome in my house. You must be strong and continue my work until time for you to come home my son!" As Michael laid there his grandmother and mother seemed to just vanish into nothing. Nadeema put her hand in Michael's hand. She looked at him with a smile on her face. Michael looked up and asked,

"You, she didn't tell me if she felt pain when it happened." The door burst opened and two soldiers quickly walked in to the room. They were dressed in combat gear and walked over to Michael. They looked at a picture of Michael with a disappointed look on their faces when the picture looked nothing like him. One of the soldiers hurried over to the window and looked out.

The people on the street below were still in a state of panic and shock. The soldier at the window looked over his shoulder at Michael with a tear in his eye. He closed his eyes and turned back towards the window. Michael slowly got up out of the bed and stumbled as he tried to walk. Nadeema was nervous and quickly grabbed Michael under his arm to help steady him. She was afraid that once Michael had seen what Balentar had done, the damage would be worse with his holy rage. Nadeema stepped in front of Michael and put her hands on his chest and smiled softly saying,

"Michael; father is watching in sorrow as Balentar has taken the life of an innocent. You must understand that what Balentar has done was to provoke you into a confrontation which would only cause more innocent people to go home to be with father before it is their time." Michael closed his eyes and bowed his head as he turned and sat down on the bed. He held on to her hands and wept as Nadeema kneeled down in front of him. She put her arms around him and comforted him.

Michael whispered,

"I understand and know now what it is that I've not known up until now. I must see what it is that Balentar has done to the innocent." Nadeema stood up and allowed Michael to rise and go over to the window. The soldier couldn't believe what he was seeing as he stood at the window staring out at the destruction on the street below. Michael stood next to the soldier and looked down at the street below. He put his hand on the soldiers shoulder and told him,

"I know that all seems lost," as he spoke he noticed Balentar standing across the street smiling at him. He gritted his teeth and turned to leave but Nadeema stopped him,

"That's exactly what he wants you to do. He wants you to fight him when you're not ready." Michael felt helpless and yet he felt a strong sense of inner strength growing inside of him with every breath. Nadeema felt the strength which was growing inside of Michael. She smiled and told him,

"The feelings you are experiencing, is that of the powers which you have always possessed. Michael my love, you have always been upon the Earth to protect and defend the reputation of Heaven and to keep the balance of good and evil in alignment. Now the scales have been off set when Balentar and the unholy dark ones escaped from Hell." Michael smiled and shook his head putting his arms around Nadeema and squeezing her, he whispered in her ear,

"I know, and now it's time to send him back down to Hell, where he and his kind belong." Nadeema felt Michael start to vibrate as he loosened his grip and stepped back away from her. Michael bowed his head and a glow surrounded him. The hospital gown seemed to disappear as a golden suit of armor had appeared covering his body. A purple cloak covering his back had a golden cross and swords crisscrossed behind it. The inscription on the cross said,

"GOD'S JUDGEMENT SHALL BE SWIFT." A golden shield, spear and a sword appeared in the corner of the room. Michael walked over and picked them up and turned back towards Nadeema. The soldier looked fearfully at Michael because he'd never seen anything like what had just happened with Michael. Nadeema smiled and kneeled down on one knee bowing her head. She remained there until Michael kneeled down in front of her and lifted her head kissing her lips and caressing her cheek. The two of them stood up and looked over at the soldier who'd seen Nadeema kneel and he also kneeled. He was weeping and asked Michael to forgive him for being afraid and to give him the strength to regain his courage.

Michael walked over and placed his hand on the soldiers head asking him his name. The soldier with tears in his eyes slowly looked up at Michael with a quivery voice said,

"My name is Jack, Jack Patton." Michael smile and reached down taking his hand he helped him to his feet. The soldier stood there looking down as Michael spoke the words of the prayer of strength and courage. Michael lifted Jack's head to look into his eyes. Jack's eye's shifted side to side as Michael looked at him. Jack felt an overwhelming feeling of courage which he hadn't felt for so long. Nadeema slowly walked over and stood next to Michael. She looked at Jack,

"Jack, the father has held back what you've had the whole time." Nadeema paused as she turned and walked over to the window and looked out at Balentar who was still standing across from the hospital. Standing there smiling with the kind of smile that sent chills down her spine. She turned her head and looked over at Michael,

"It's time my love. The Lords work waits for no one or no want to be ruler of what belongs to the father." Then she turned back to the window and started smiling back at Balentar which made him furious. Michael put his hand out to Jack and nodded his head. Jack took Michael's hand and felt as if he was God himself was with him. Michael turned towards the door and took a deep breath. As he took a step towards the door, the door opened by it's self. Michael walked out into the hall way followed by Jack. As Jack stepped through the door way, he stopped and looked back at Nadeema,

"Thank you, thank you very much for everything. I feel like a brand new person, a brand new soldier for God." Nadeema smiled and Jack patted the door jam with his palm and walked down the hall way behind Michael. As Michael walked down the hall, everyone stepped aside and gave him clear passage. They didn't know if they were afraid of him or astonished by the apparel he was wearing. When Michael and Jack reached the elevator, the door opened and five soldiers were standing inside. They looked at Michael and pushed back tightly against the wall and allowed Michael and Jack to enter.

Their eyes never left Michael the whole way down to the ground floor. As the door opened Michael stepped out and turned to the soldiers and looked at them,

"Join me and make father proud." The soldiers stepped forward off of the elevator and ask if Michael had a plan of attack. Jack stepped over in front of them with a serious look on his face he answered for Michael,

"The plan is gentlemen; we take care of business the good old fashion way. We flank attack and cover fire during the assault. Michael is the boss man and we must protect the boss at all cost no matter he must succeed. And should we not survive, we will live in glory." Michael went to each of them placing his hand on the shoulder of each of them saying,

"May God be with you and protect you from all harm as you glorify him in battle." Michael turned and walked through the front door drawing his sword from its sheath. Jack and the other soldiers made their way through a side door and around behind Balentar. With Michael standing in front of the hospital Balentar kept his attention focused on Michael as the soldiers got into position to cover Michael.

Balentar keeping his eyes on Michael moving parallel with him as Michael walked towards Pinkie and Linda. He asked if they were injured but they were more scared than anything. Michael looked down at Malone who laid lifeless on the ground. A tear fell from his eye and landed on Malone's lips. As if a charge of electricity surged through her, her heart started beating and she gasped. Michael told Pinkie and Linda to get her to safety. As they got up and made their way back into the door they came out of, Michael looked at Balentar with a solid stare.

He walked slowly with his shield up in front of his chest to protect him from Balentar. Michael looked over at the soldiers who were in position he ask Balentar,

"What gives you the right to try and take what never belonged to you. Only my father your father has that right." Balentar grew angry and a ball of fire formed in his hand throwing it at Michael. The fire ball hit Michaels shield exploding into little sparks. Michael pointed his sword at Balentar and laughed at him,

"Is that the best you can do; apparently you don't understand plain English. You can not win; you will never win because God protects and shields those whom love him from evil such as your self." Balentar started throwing one fire ball after another at Michael. The soldiers behind Balentar opened fire on Balentar hitting him several times. The bullet holes healed as fast as they were created. Balentar turned and blasted the soldiers with fire balls incinerating two of the soldiers into ashes and burning Jack and the other soldiers so bad they were screaming out in pain.

Michael raised up his sword to the sky, storm clouds moved in overhead. Balentar looked nervous as he look up at the clouds. Lightning came out of the sky and into Michaels sword as he stood there glowing with a brilliant beautiful orange light surrounding his body. Balentar angered yet frightened of Michael rapidly threw fire balls at Michael as Michael walked towards him. Every fire ball he had thrown at Michael seemed to dissolve as Michael pointed his sword at them.

Balentar pointed at a mail box ripping it from its anchors and hurling it at Michael. Michael put his shield in front of him and the mail box deflected away from him slamming against an overturned truck next to him. Michael pointed at the mail box which lifted off of the ground and pointed at Balentar. The mail box hurled at Balentar striking him so hard he looked as if he was glued to it. When he landed against the pile of rubble; Balentar didn't move for a few minutes. Michael thought that the fight was over and he started walking towards Balentar. When he was within feet of him; Balentar moved.

As the mail box fell away from Balentar Michael kept his shield tightly against him and placed his sword in front of him. Balentar had blood coming from his nose and ears. His eyes glowed red and he laid there for a few seconds before getting up. The whole time Michael watched and waited for him to try something else against him. Balentar looked up at Michael winded and acting hurt,

"Go ahead all mighty Michael; go ahead and sleigh the only demon who'd ever escaped from the prison which God created. But just remember this; when I escaped the first of many whom fell at my feet was your own brother. So go ahead thrust your sword and send me back." Michael placed his sword to the throat of Balentar. When Balentar smiled; he knew something wasn't right because he gave up too easy. Balentar looked over at the end of the street, a look of fear fell over his face. Michael looked over and seen a thin built man dressed all in black carrying a staff of ivory with a large diamond on the top standing there.

Balentar pleaded with Michael as not to let him take him away. Michael stood there while the stranger walked slowly towards them. The strangers face was hard as stone and his eyes were dark and cold. Michael wasn't sure where he knew him from, but the feeling of concern ran through his body like a freight train. When he was about ten feet away from him Michael he looked at Michael then at Balentar and took a deep breath,

"How dare you; you putrid; poor excuse for a damned soul. I have never lost one of my; well let's just say; no one has ever escaped from damnation." He pointed at Balentar and tilted his head back taking a deep breath from know where the sky grew dark and the wind grew strong. He put his arms straight out to the side and lightning started coming out of his back striking behind him. He tilted his head forwards looking down at the ground in front of him. As he slowly lifted his head his eyes were glowing red and his voice sounded disfigured as he spoke.

"Balentar you will regret everything you have done without my consent." Then he looked at Michael and started speaking to him with an occasional glance at Balentar,

"Michael; most holy of all warriors, do you have any objections if I take care of Balentar personally. The harm he has done is regrettable but can not be undone; unless he;" looking up with his head tilted to the side, "will do as he always does. But never the less Balentar will pay dearly for his disobedience and insolence. This matter will be dealt with swiftly and precisely with no leniency and this I guarantee." Michael drew back his sword from Balentar, placing it back into its sheath and stepped away from him.

The stranger moved over in front of Balentar. He chuckled as the fear Balentar felt towards him fed his hunger and need to make him feel superior. As he stooped down in front of Balentar; he put his hand on Balentar's forehead. The stranger started chanting over and over as the strangers hand began glowing bright red. Balentar started screaming and fazed in and out of human form and into his true demon form. After a few moments Balentar remained in demon form and his body started to glow with an intense blinding light. You could hear an unbearable shrilling sound as Balentar's body slowly vanished and the light and sound dissipated.

The stranger stood back up and turned towards Michael who'd drawn his sword from its sheath and put his shield up in front of him. The stranger put his hands behind his back cupping them together and chuckling as he told Michael,

"Michael; do not fear what you have never feared before." Michael didn't trust him and kept his guard up. The stranger looked up and the sky cleared. His eyes and voice returned to normal. Nadeema left the hospital room and joined Michael outside. The stranger seen Nadeema walking towards them and took a fearful breath.

Nadeema walked over to Michael and stood with him at his side. Michael lowered his sword pointing it towards the ground. The stranger spoke to Nadeema,

"Well; well; well; Nadeema the one and only Nadeema. I knew one day we'd see each other again.

How long has it been; one; two thousand years?" Nadeema looked at him with distain and repulsion. He chuckled as he turned and walked slowly away. Michael said to him,

"I'll be watching over my fathers creations; protecting those whom are weak in spirit. And one day bring home those whom are lost." Michael and Nadeema watched as he walked away saying,

"Don't worry Michael; I'll stay in touch."

THE END

Ronald A. Turner